Walking in Paradise

WALKING IN PARADISE
LIBBY CREELMAN

[handwritten inscription: Stratford Sept 23/00 / For Heidi, / all the best! / (signature)]

The Porcupine's Quill

CANADIAN CATALOGUING IN PUBLICATION DATA

Creelman, Elizabeth, 1957–
Walking in paradise

ISBN 0-88984-216-7

I. Title.

PS8555.R434W34 2000   C813'.6   C00-932083-0
PR9199.3.C683W34 2000

Canadä

Published by The Porcupine's Quill,
68 Main Street, Erin, Ontario NOB 1TO.
Readied for the press by John Metcalf; copy edited by Doris Cowan.
Typeset in Minion, printed on Zephyr Antique laid,
and bound at The Porcupine's Quill Inc.

This is a work of fiction. Any resemblance of characters to persons,
living or dead, is purely coincidental.

Represented in Canada by the Literary Press Group.
Trade orders are available from General Distribution Services.

We acknowledge the support of the Ontario Arts Council,
and the Canada Council for the Arts for our publishing program.
The financial support of the Government of Canada
through the Book Publishing Industry Development Program
is also gratefully acknowledged.

1 2 3 4 · 02 01 00

For my parents

* * *

I would like to thank the Newfoundland and Labrador Arts Council
and the Canada Council for their financial assistance.

I also want to thank and acknowledge
Helen Porter, Janet Fraser, Stan Dragland,
and all members of the Newfoundland Writers' Guild
for their support and criticism.

Contents

THREE WEEKS

THE THREE OF THEM left Connecticut on the same morning, in a heat wave. Rosanna and Mike were subdued, already sweating. They waited as their mother turned the key in the front door lock, then as she stepped back and gave them one last look of worry and regret. She was wearing too much make-up and new clothes, carrying new suitcases. She told them she didn't want to say who she was going off with in case it didn't work out. Anyway, this time it was no one they knew.

'I'll call every day,' she said, looking at Rosanna. 'I promise. Then I'll see you both, right back here, in three weeks.'

Mike couldn't help laughing. 'Where did you think we were going, Mom?'

'I *know* where. The house in Maine.'

'There's no phone there, Mom. Remember?' Rosanna said, hoping there was still a chance she might not have to go. On either side of them the neighbours' sprinklers clicked round and round with that harmless tinny sound of summer.

Her mother lowered her suitcases and reached inside the collar of her blouse to rearrange something, briefly exposing her hard, straight collarbones. Then she kissed them both.

Inside her shorts pocket Rosanna's fingers coiled around her last joint, so feather-light it seemed possible to lose it, even if it never left her pocket.

'Thanks, kids,' her mother said gently. 'Thanks for doing this.'

* * *

Their cousin Peter met them in the trodden-down grass outside the kitchen door, bare-chested and grinning. He was as skinny at twenty-four as he had been at eight. He'd let his hair grow and it was pulled back now into a strangled ponytail on his bare back.

A shadow passed inside the old farmhouse, and a noise: something dropped or bumped into, then a murmured curse.

'How's the asparagus?' Mike asked.

Peter held a hand out waist high and announced, 'Up to here on me already.' He paused. 'But I didn't know you were bringing a twelve-year-old.'

'Sixteen, asshole,' Rosanna said, just as a young woman appeared in the doorway behind Peter, who turned, his face bright, saying, 'Haven't met Debbie, have you?'

She had short hair bundled in soft curls and a flawless face that seemed to carry with it a certain oblique vigour and influence. Rosanna could tell that Mike disliked her immediately, even before she used her stomach to prod open the screen door and emerge barefoot into the sunlight, her arms and legs covered in lilac speckles.

Peter placed his hand on her belly and said to Mike, 'Three more months, bud. Three more months and you're looking at Daddy.'

'She's not fat, Mike. She's pregnant,' Rosanna said as they darted up the field behind the house so Mike could get his bearings after meeting Debbie and witnessing the change to the house. She was painting it purple. *Lilac.*

'That kitchen's going to be hard on my head,' warned Mike.

'I saw some yellow paint too,' Rosanna offered, wanting to pacify her brother, but also, to somehow elevate herself to his level of conversation.

'I can't wait for Louie to show.'

Though this was the first Rosanna had heard of anyone named Louie, she said, 'No kidding.'

'Don't copycat,' said Mike, who had always been fast. He reached over and popped his open hand across the back of her head so that her hair tossed into her eyes and she plunged into her next step. But it was a long shot from the old days.

When she lifted her head again they were just nearing the vegetable garden at the top of the field. Beyond the garden was a small grove of hardwoods, and beyond that, a second field. Rosanna hadn't been up there in years.

'If you say one word – one word, Rosanna – about what I have to tell you now, I'll go bananas. Do you read me?'

'Yeah.'

'Positive?'

'Yeah!'

'You're staying in the house with Peter and *her* –'

'Since when?'

'Since there's only that one other bedroom and blah-blah-blah. And Louie, whenever he fucking gets his ass up here –'

'Where's he coming from?'

'His girlfriend. She's breaking up with him, basically. Anyway, my point is, Louie and I have been invited to stay in the bunkroom.'

'How 'bout I stay in the bunkroom and you and Louie stay in the house?'

'Ha ha. So we're clear on the sleeping arrangements?'

'Where's your plants? *The asparagus.*'

Mike gave her a fierce look, unsure of the extent to which he was being mocked, and she moved a step away from him, her shoulders drawing inwards.

'You keep away from those plants, Rosanna. You're not in on it, do you read me?'

'So where do I do my shopping around here?'

'You gotta be the biggest pothead I know. Sixteen fucking years old. Jesus fucking …'

She stopped abruptly in the path beside the pole beans and let him continue marching on, shaking his head. He halted after a few feet and turned back to look at her with a quizzical expression, as though she'd just asked him something. He was losing his train of thought.

She put her hand out. 'That joint we smoked on the way up was my last.'

'Already? You're out already?'

They gave up talking. Rosanna gazed back down at the farmhouse, which leaned to the west and was surrounded by a field intersected at odd angles by ragged stone walls. The house itself was a small cape with pitched roof and weathered, nearly white, clapboards. Black shutters had long ago fallen off and were stacked now in an attic corner, the paint lifting like the wings of dark moths. The house gave the impression, despite its recent history, of tidy domesticity and security. At the east end, attached to the small kitchen, was the woodshed – housing the bunkhouse, a 1970s addition – and attached to that, the gigantic barn. Both woodshed and barn were covered in rough shingles. There was no running water, electricity, or telephone. The place had belonged to

Rosanna's great-grandfather and then her grandmother on her father's side.

Peter and Debbie had been living in the house since June, when they put the plants in – both what Rosanna could see here in the garden, and whatever illegal bounty was now flourishing up in the other field. Rosanna had been hoping Mike might take her up there now, but it didn't look that way. For her, she realized, that field and those plants would be strictly off limits.

It was hot. Insects were knocking themselves out in the corn and summer squash, zucchini and beets. There had been a lot of rain recently and every plant was green-swollen, luxurious under the blue sky, growing helter-skelter in all directions. The field swept out from beneath Rosanna's feet, then moved on down towards the farmhouse, circling round it before moving off to meet the dirt road. Heat waves were being cast up from the earth, engulfing the house, the woodshed and barn, Rosanna and Mike.

They had beets and zucchini for supper, and some dry cornbread Peter had made, eating at the kitchen table beside the grubby-paned window. What Rosanna liked best about this place was that in her lifetime, at least, there had never been a central female force maintaining it. It was always grimy, damp, cool, even in summer. The landscape outside might be basking in reproduction and heat, but here in the kitchen, where they were presently too stoned to say much, the temperature was ideal.

At last Peter looked at Mike and said, 'Come on,' and without another word they rose and left.

The kitchen door remained open, jammed on the flattened grass. Someone had detached the spring from the door frame, and Rosanna watched it swing from the open door. She lit another joint. Mike had given her a small supply, already rolled, which irked her because she liked to roll her own. It was one of his many ways of exercising control over her.

Debbie approached, smelling of oil paint. Her drum-tight stomach brushed Rosanna's shoulder. The thing she was wearing looked suspiciously like a nightie. It was hiked up in front on account of her stomach and if anyone had been interested, they could have easily seen what she wore as underwear.

It was careful work placing the joint between Debbie's fingers, since Debbie seemed to have trouble holding her hand steady. It was something Rosanna did reluctantly, anyway.

Then a shadow fell across the doorway and Debbie dropped the joint.

'Fuck, fuck, fuck,' Debbie said, as she lowered herself without bending and began crawling beneath the table in search of the lit joint.

'Door was open,' he said to Rosanna. 'Sorry if I scared you.' Then he glanced around the room. He was dark, not from the sun, but naturally, as though he'd been standing in the shadows of dense foliage too long and had grown to resemble his surroundings. When Rosanna saw the chunky class ring he wore, she experienced a sudden sinking; it seemed impossible to reconcile her friends and high school life with what she was just beginning now with these strangers.

He asked her something, but she knew that the sound of her own voice might be a destructive thing. She needed to erase her existence from this kitchen.

As she passed through the low doorway and across the sloping floorboards, she considered her hair and clothes, the way she walked, aware that he was likely observing her. She headed for the sofa.

When she opened her eyes she was still high, still on the sofa. Her first thought was: *only moments have passed,* her second: *underneath these cushions there are my father's old Playboy magazines.*

Debbie was making room for herself beside Rosanna's legs, saying, 'That happens to me sometimes.' Then she produced a long, laboured sigh. 'They went up back, Louie. Want me to show you?'

They were gone, and although it was what she had wished for, loneliness flooded Rosanna until she hurt, like she was only a rag dipped in a puddle of brown liquid so foul she'd wake tomorrow swollen.

She missed her mother. She missed home.

There was no television here, no pool, friends, malls. No summer days of hanging out, doing nothing with girls she had known forever, girls with whom late at night, smoked up, a specific demented look or code word could bring on hysterical laughter. These people – her brother, a cousin, two strangers – were much older, in their twenties. It was frightening being with people you didn't know. They seemed to be a different species of animal. At any given moment you had no idea what thoughts they were having. You could wake in the middle of the night and have no knowledge of what they dreamed. Maybe you were in their dreams, but doing what?

Or they might be awake, you just wouldn't know. They might be touching one another.

Opposite the sofa was the fireplace and beside that, the brick oven, its cast-iron door marked, JACOB KIMBALL, PORTLAND, ME., though Rosanna did not have to read this to know it was there. The door was slightly ajar, and Rosanna could see where inside the oven Debbie had placed her paint tins and brushes.

She rolled face first into the back of the sofa. Its upholstery smelled of burning wood and old trunks. It smelled of the last century.

'You blacked out?' Mike was saying.

It was dark now in the house.

'Go away.'

'Don't get stupid, Rosanna.'

'Shut up. Go away.'

He punched her shoulder. The sofa springs creaked beneath her and someone in the room inhaled sharply. 'Rosanna, go to bed. We're gonna go look for a bar, all right, so just go to bed and don't smoke any more or else.'

'Maybe your sister wants to come,' Louie suggested. Rosanna figured he was standing just inside the doorway; she couldn't see him where she lay.

'Or else what?' she asked.

'She's fucking sixteen, Louie. Look at her.'

Rosanna woke the following morning bored, even before she stepped from her bed. She felt jailed. She felt overlooked. Mike had made it clear he didn't want her going anywhere near those plants. As though she were such a maniac she'd go up there and start tearing them all to shreds and stuffing them in her mouth.

The day passed, and then others, hushed and uneventful. Rosanna suspected that everyone was somewhere inside, either in the house or woodshed or barn, yet they remained hidden, as though involved with mysterious work forbidden to her. She knew there was nothing to caring for the plants at this stage, unless watching them grow counted for something. It took her a while to realize that everyone was spending a lot of time asleep.

Not long into the morning, she would lock her doors and lie on her bed and light a joint. Her room was at the front of the house and had once been the parlour. The plaster walls were white, the wainscoting below muddy green. Fortunately, Debbie seemed uninterested in painting this room. The fireplace opposite Rosanna's bed was surrounded by modestly carved panelling, lending it a plain, dignified look that Rosanna found soothing.

If she rolled her head on the slab of blankets that served as her pillow, and gazed through light as white and calm as the inside of a blown egg shell, she could see her belongings dumped at the foot of the corner cabinet behind whose noble, ancient glass someone years ago had placed a collection of rocks and what were believed to be several arrowheads and chunks of petrified wood. Both the cabinet and simple fireplace opening Rosanna examined over and over as she lay, listening for sounds, for hours. The weight of her high kept her low, her spirits muffled. She felt tortured by a desire to surface, to search for something, yet at the same time felt safe in this room because there was nothing in here to discover.

Once or twice a day she grew curious enough to venture out, though always avoiding Debbie, who, without ever leaving the house, seemed to spend more time awake than anyone else as she travelled from bedroom to living room to kitchen and back again with quick mincing steps that made her appear both officious and childlike.

Rosanna usually met Louie in the kitchen. She'd only be in there a minute, rooting for something in the cooler, when he'd come in through the woodshed entrance. He'd start talking to her and ask if she wanted to go for a walk and she would pretend she hadn't heard him and hurry back to her room. Once he even knocked on her door and spoke her name, but she ignored that too.

In the late afternoon she would wake from a nap she had never intended on taking, and hear voices again in the house. Groggy, she would turn to the window beside her bed and stare out at the hot humid air that met the landscape as though it would swallow it. The sky was blue-hazy with heat, yet there seemed no plant or insect that could suffer in this climate. Trees, saplings, grass, garden vegetables, thickets of vines, shrubs and wildflowers, all stood deceptively motionless, but growing nevertheless. Tricksters, vegetative reproduction: their growth was palpable. She knew that she was somehow witness to it, though powerless to see it with her eyes.

Sometimes at night a light rain fell and she would wake in her bed and picture it landing drop by drop on the narrow-fingered leaves of the plants up in the forbidden field blackened now by rain clouds. Pattering in ringlets on the soil surrounding each bulging stalk.

And then she would hear from within the house the creak of a voice or furniture, a sudden ping or muffled word, and she would turn onto her stomach and dig her head beneath the mildewed blankets.

At the end of each day, still a strong light in the sky after their meal of boiled vegetables and toast, they grouped in the cool, stale air of the living room – originally the winter kitchen – and smoked up. Someone would suggest a trip to Shape's Lake to clean off, and Rosanna would wait, anxious to go, but in the end they only argued over when to begin harvesting, then staggered off to bed.

Rosanna sat on the raised hearth, a good distance from her brother, since his mood, as the days passed, grew increasingly jumpy. The ashes and clumps of charcoal in the hearth behind her gave off a sharp metallic aroma. The mineral remains of trees. The smell of wood ghosts, cold, sad. Growing and living that would never be again.

'I thought I heard a helicopter today,' Mike said one evening. He flicked a piece of oatmeal cookie across the room. It landed neatly in Rosanna's hair.

'Fuck you, Mike,' she said.

Peter was looking wearily at Mike. 'They don't go over with helicopters any more. I think I mentioned that to you about eighty-one times already.'

At this, Debbie giggled, the sound of it a rutty laziness that Peter appeared unable to resist. He rose and began moving across the room towards her, taking, it seemed to Rosanna, hours. As though he were savouring the passage over, the anticipation.

Mike shifted with impatience, then shot several pieces of cookie at Rosanna.

'Look at the mess you're making,' Louie said, annoyed. 'You're a pig.'

Peter arrived at Debbie's feet and lowered himself to his knees and took up one of her legs. She was wearing shorts, loose and negligible. He lifted the leg, straight as a broomstick, higher and higher, until it nearly touched her nose. It was clear to everyone that, pregnant or not, she had impressive flexibility.

When he released the leg it dropped like a log but he caught it, a whisper above the floorboards. Then he picked up the other leg and began tossing both, one at a time, up and down like scissors. Debbie sat smiling remotely.

Mike rose. Louie was only a minute behind him. They were gone.

'Right here,' Peter suggested after a while. He had Debbie's legs raised, but her knees were bent now, pinned wing-like on either side of her.

'I don't like that,' Debbie said. She sounded winded.

He allowed her knees to drop slightly, no more than an inch. 'Right here, Debbie. What do you say?'

Debbie looked across the room with mild curiosity. 'We're not alone, stupid.'

'Come on. Right here.'

'Where'd your brother go?' Debbie asked Rosanna, who shrugged. 'And that really gorgeous guy he's got with him?'

Peter sat back on his heels. 'You mean the one with the ugly face?'

Debbie laughed generously, then spoke in a voice that seemed to drive Peter nuts. 'He's gorgeous. Black hair, black eyes. If he was mine, I'd dress him in deep blues and marine greens. Every single day of his life.' She tried to sit up but Peter immediately restrained her. She punched him twice on his shoulder, still teasing, still smiling. 'What do you think, Rosanna? But I guess you're kinda young yet. Aren't you?'

Rosanna glanced at Debbie, reluctant to enter into a conversation with her. She turned her attention to her toes, spreading them over the floorboards and lifting her arches, pretending to be too preoccupied with her feet to have heard Debbie's question.

But Debbie was suddenly suspicious, her resentment of Rosanna descending out of the clear blue. 'You *did* notice him. What a sneaky rat she is, Peter.' She put her hands on Peter to push him off, but he was heavy and determined. She said again, 'I don't like that.'

Then she closed her eyes, forgetting Rosanna. Her head dropped forward with a languid nod. When Rosanna realized Peter's jeans were unbound, the waistline slipping down his white hips, she felt like an idiot, like a child.

Had the two of them dumped her by the side of a country road they could not have abandoned her more thoroughly than they did now. Rosanna swallowed and slipped her hands beneath her thighs. Her palms were cold where they lay over the gritty bricks, the tops of her hands warm where they met her own skin. Her mother would want her to leave the room immediately. Even Mike would want that.

Several mornings later Mike, Louie and Peter headed up to the second field with uneasy agreement and two chainsaws between them. Rosanna watched from inside the farmhouse until they had disappeared through the stand of trees separating the two fields.

'This constant scared shitless business,' Debbie said, slumped on the sofa. 'It'll end once they get the harvest in.' She pushed herself upwards and her voice grew stronger. 'Businessmen, man, I tell ya. They think they're soooo important. Soooo grown-up. Bringing in the bacon. They crack me up.'

For over an hour they listened to the distant whine of the chainsaws. Then Debbie put together a picnic lunch and invited Rosanna to help her carry it.

Mike looked up as they approached and Rosanna saw the crippling fear cross his face before he recognized them. He was that wound up. Instinctively, she kept away from him. The field had originally been used for grazing cattle – too hilly for cultivation – and was now nearly disguised by the invasion of small spruce and pine. But Rosanna, curious and relieved to be here at last, cast her eyes over the landscape and easily picked out the plants: an unmistakable nutty shade of green, so plainly non-native, uniform in height, and mostly bud, which she knew, of course, was the whole point.

Half lay fallen, already cut. Louie was dragging them off the field into a dark feathery heap in the shade.

Along one edge of the field ranks of steeplebush and meadowsweet were blooming and here Debbie threw out the blanket she'd taken from the bed she and Peter shared. She set out the fluffernutter sandwiches, popcorn, cold water, hot boiled vegetables. Then she sat and waited.

'Didn't we just have breakfast?' Peter complained, flopping down on the blanket and picking up a sandwich.

'Oh, Louie,' Debbie called out in a voice sing-song, motherly and strained. 'Oh, Mike.'

'Take a break, guys,' Peter said. Then, 'Are ya deaf?'

The mood was tense. Rosanna figured it had been tense all morning. She wondered if they'd notice if she rose now and went off back down to the house. Yes, they would. Peter had felt the plants could go another week, easily. Mike and Louie thought the time was now. Why wait for disaster. For hammering rain. For helicopters moving over the countryside like gigantic roving eyes.

Debbie suddenly glanced at Rosanna with a look both beseeching and confiding. As though they were pals. But what could Rosanna do? How could she entice Mike and Louie to come take up a sandwich and express gratitude to Debbie?

At last Debbie rose to her feet in several distinct stages and went into the hot field, her quick short steps ill-fitting outside the dark farmhouse. Both Rosanna and Peter strained to hear her words as she leaned over Mike, then Louie, her hand on the lower centre of his drenched back. Rosanna watched the three straggle towards her. She noticed how soft and droopy their clothes had grown through lack of washing, yet the memory of each person's individual body shape seemed present in their clothing. The effect was personal, intimate. Rosanna realized her own clothes must look that way, too.

Neither Louie nor Mike seemed inclined to share the blanket but sat just beyond it. After several minutes Mike grew comfortable in the shade. White fluff ringed his lips. When Rosanna crossed behind him he spun suddenly on his rear and whipped a leg into her path. He grinned as she went over, spilling her water on the blanket. The steamy scent of wet dirty cloth rose into the air.

And then he couldn't stop harassing her, like a puppy driven to tearing furniture or ankles. He tripped her, shoved her, tossed and rubbed food into her face and hair, down the neck of her shirt.

Rosanna waited it out, knowing that any attempt to escape would be a mistake. She sat cross-legged, head bowed, until Mike had flicked the last of his vegetables onto her lap.

In the silence she heard a blue jay and looked up. Except for Mike, they were all watching her. Peter looked mesmerized; Louie either curious or amused; and Debbie so jolly her face nearly rippled with it. A flood of hate for them swept through Rosanna. In her mind's eye she watched herself closing the distance between herself and Debbie, ripping out great gobs of her hair, tearing those delicate cheeks, kicking that belly. Hurting her in such a way that Mike's actions would be utterly eclipsed.

But she got dizzy when she stood quickly and that forced her to wait and by then she'd lost her courage. She turned to go, accepting that Mike could make her short passage across the field to those trees a miserable experience.

Bodies shifted behind her, footsteps pounded, there was a rush of movement, a grunt, a thud. Rosanna walked on, waiting for Mike to tackle her. When he didn't, she glanced back to find Louie and Mike rolling in the dry grass with such a yearning to destroy each other they might have been reading her thoughts. They might have leapt from her mind. As though she might reclaim her feelings and return them to their secret place, she took a step towards them, then stopped, her hands at her sides. Slowly, she gave those feelings up. She let Mike and Louie keep them.

She gazed at the hazy liquid sky, the evergreens ringing the field, at Debbie and Peter posed like dolls in a pile of toy plates and cups and one filthy blanket. Where her heart should have been there was an object the size of a plum or hard-boiled egg. It had always interfered with her breathing.

The energy with which Mike and Louie first went at each other began to slacken. There was a rush of wrestling movement, an abrupt ugly pause as Louie pinned and held Mike, then another rush, a rearranging of limbs and suddenly Rosanna remembered Debbie's knees pinned away from her body and Peter as he knelt quickening against her: once started, nothing could have stopped him. She saw them screwing in their bed, in the woods, on that blanket. And somehow, each time, Rosanna was responsible.

Louie shook Mike, though Mike lay surrendered on his back on the ground, then rose over him and shouted, 'You're a pig.' He was panting, his hair bunched over his forehead. 'If I had a sister I would like her. I would take care of her. You're disgusting. You know that?'

They searched for Rosanna for hours, or at least Louie, Debbie and Peter searched for her, called for her, walked right by her. When Mike found her, after dark, it was only because he chose to. She was hiding where she had always hidden. He crawled up into the small space over the roof of the inside privy at the back of the barn where she crouched, hidden by rolls of chicken wire, a stack of metal buckets and very little light.

'Anyone had a dump recently?' he joked.

'No, but Debbie has had a number of pisses. Talked to herself, too, but I couldn't hear what. Something about Peter.'

He looked at her. Her face was dusty and had that moist look that couldn't have been just from sweat. She'd been crying. He took care of her, didn't he? Of course he did. Shit, looked like Louie wanted the job though. The thought softened him to Louie. And to Rosanna.

He helped her down, then the two of them returned to the kitchen where Mike sat at the kitchen table looking out at the first stars while Rosanna made a jam sandwich. He wanted to say something to her, but what? He tried to imagine what their mother might say. The way she might at this moment console Rosanna.

When Debbie started through the doorway he snarled, and she turned back, looking indignant and crushed. He didn't want anyone coming near Rosanna tonight.

They tied the plants up in the barn. Mike invited Rosanna to help and stood by her, at least the first day, showing her how to strip the greasy, rose-coloured buds and discard the curled leaves, reminding her over and over not to touch her eyes with her hands. At best, from a distance – outdoors or in the house – the smell was sweet, like cloves, like Christmas cookies, honeyed and luscious. She lay in her bed at night and it lingered in the air above her as a reminder of her day, standing across from Louie, his class ring flashing in the gloomy light as he stripped buds as thick as his thumb.

Inside the barn, the doors closed and everyone silent, the smell was more pungent, rank, skunk-like. Even Peter seemed uneasy. Rosanna watched each time as Debbie, though she should have known better, put a finger into an eye and moments later – the door banging open, Peter cursing – went reeling outside where she stood gagging not far from the house.

But even this, Rosanna liked. The close, overwhelming odour, the illicit risk. The possessing of these forbidden plants and all that the soil and sun and rain had given them.

The second day they quit early, weak and careless from one head rush after another, the sticky organic dust having found its way into every crack of skin and clothing.

They were the only people at Shape's Lake and swam naked. Peter moved slowly nearer Debbie in a silent game of his own that the rest tried to ignore.

Rosanna avoided everyone, submerging and opening her eyes, forcing her mind to narrow on a single pinpoint of thought: let the others drown and disappear. Disappear, disappear, she began to chant aloud, forgetting she was underwater, so that bubbles came out of her mouth and went rushing to the surface like round, explicit signals.

She waited until everyone was out, then hurried to shore into the circle of pine trees where she had undressed, stepping over needles perfumed and spongy. A squirrel hidden from view began to natter on at her: fearful, annoyed, curious. A woodpecker hammered bark with a momentum and beat that suggested he'd not taken a rest in years. A pinched shriek from Debbie shot past and was gone. Rosanna heard all this with a precision that touched her, though she did not know it.

She had her shirt on and was balancing on one foot, poised to step into her underpants, when she heard footsteps and realized suddenly several things: she was half dressed and wet, her clothes were dirty, she would be starting grade eleven in only a week.

Louie was passing, on his way to the road.

She stepped quickly into her underpants and began yanking them up. Pine needles on the soles of her feet dropped into the crotch. She knew that Louie had stopped, that he could not resist noticing this. She swiped at the needles, gave up and pulled at her underpants but they rolled under and tangled on her wet thighs.

'Wait. Don't,' he said, coming over. He leaned down and lifted the crotch at the sides and shook it until it was cleared of debris. Then he moved his fingers around one of her thighs, then the other, thoughtfully and with his face averted, like a person picking a raffle ticket from a hat, and untangled her underwear. Despite some distant, dreary mortification, she waited to see if he would pull them up.

As the squirrel rounded a trunk only a few feet away, its voice gone, its tail swishing, its need to see getting the better of it, she stared at Louie's head bent over her, at the tight curls of black hair flashing with oil and water. Here was a proximity to something she had not planned on. He was a man. And he was very near. I'm only sixteen, she wanted to remind him.

She thought he would say, 'What are you afraid of?' because that's what boys had said before, but he said nothing.

It was only when she realized her underpants were stained an ugly yellow that she blushed. Louie straightened with an expression she could not read. As he walked off across the needle floor she considered how remarkable it was that his breath should have felt so hot.

When she reached the road they were all there, waiting for her, reluctant to get back into the stuffy car; instead, roaming over the road which had recently been paved. Fresh, oily chunks of tar were crumbling into gutters already caked with pine needles, leaves, twigs, slippery amphibians. When no one would meet Rosanna's eye, she knew they had been witness to Louie helping her with her underwear in the pine woods clearing.

Peter got in behind the wheel and Debbie slid in beside him. Louie took the back and left the door open for Rosanna, who put her hand on the sun-scorched handle without feeling it.

Mike hesitated before getting in the front. After a while he began rolling down his window. 'Too much?' he asked, turning slowly, reluctant to make eye contact with his sister.

The wind was lifting Rosanna's wet hair and drying the curled tips. She said, no, not too much. She liked it, in fact.

She watched the countryside pass by, her thoughts drifting to her mother – they would all be home soon and she was glad. Her face was turned instinctively away from the other passengers. But something about the look of the trees against the distant no-colour sky gradually made her impatient. When she finally thought about Louie, she realized it would be a long courtship.

BOAT RIDE

THE MOTOR YACHT is so bulky and inelegant we could be sunning ourselves halfway up a small granite mountain. But when it rocks on the water, bound loosely to the dock by gleaming white lines, it moves with a rhythm as graceful and unobtrusive as the breathing of a sleeping child.

My mother is sprawled on her back, not far from me. One brown knee nods side to side in a small arc as she taps the deck with her naked foot and stares at the perfect cloth of blue sky.

The two of us, a Thursday morning.

My mother has spent the last half-hour fretting over Kimberly's plans to redecorate her master head: to go Japanese, with paper screens, sisal flooring, a built in saki-warmer beside a new jacuzzi. It riles her that Dad would never agree to anything so unconventional. So sexy. Though we both know what he'll say once Kimberly goes through with it: *Looks super. Honest to God, Kimberly. Super.*

She closes her eyes and runs the palm of her hand through the basin that is her abdomen. My mother has always been thin. It is impossible for her to have friends who are overweight, to eat three meals a day, to greet me without suggesting I've gained a couple pounds. I've only been here a few hours, but when she sits up now and smiles at me, she's speculating as to when I'll be getting back into that sports car Dad bought me and returning to that apartment that is really his.

'It's exhausting,' she says. 'The worrying I do on your account.'

She has a pretty face with wide-spaced eyes and button nose, an even buttery tan. After all these years, she will not stop sunning herself, hatless and unprotected. I routinely describe to her the risks of wrinkled skin and melanoma. But she maintains that everyone looks better a little brown.

'What worries you the most?' I ask, teasing her, but with affection, because I can see today how the dieting and year-round sunshine are aging her. There is a crumbled feebleness beneath her shiny surface that softens the disheartening effect her words have on me.

'For starters, Oleen, the sheer number of boyfriends you go around with.'

'I guess now would not be the time to mention two guests this week-end?'

'It's nearly lunchtime,' she says. Though lunch is an activity she will avoid if she can. 'I'm going for a drive.'

She rouses herself and moves silent as a draft into the dark interior of the boat. The wall-to-wall is soft and lovely beneath her feet. She goes barefoot here because it's clean, at least when Dad's not on board. Week-ends it's a steady job to keep grit and dirt from coming aboard. Week-ends are a free-for-all. Peanuts, potato chips, luncheon meat and lettuce, just plain sand, all underfoot. She wonders, where the hell does Nick find sand in this place?

She changes into in a baby-blue denim skirt and white jersey. She wraps a scarf turban-style around her hair, careful to avoid touching the moth orchid beside her pile of jewellery. Although she is at a loss about watering it, it thrives here, just as the florists assured her it would. Yet she persists in believing that something so exquisite must be equally vul-nerable, that ultimately it will require too much of her. I think she would be relieved if it died.

She leans into the glow of the pink teardrop lights that ring her van-ity. She is just about to pick at something on her chin when I appear behind her.

'Jesus,' my mother says.

'Sorry.'

She leans into the mirror again and scans her face. 'Maybe I should be more careful,' she concedes, then stares at me in the mirror. 'Honey, we have plenty of room but you know your father is old-fashioned. Where you're concerned at any rate.'

'I'm twenty-two. I've been having intercourse for quite some time.'

My mother sighs dramatically. She speaks in a hushed tone, as though there is some possibility of being overheard. 'Please don't speak that way! You sound like you're bragging.'

'I thought this would be a good weekend to have them. Aren't you and Dad going to Stokesley on Saturday for something?'

'Are you insane? Did he tell you that? I'm not going to any high school reunion. He can go alone.'

'He won't drive all that way alone.'

'What are their names?'

'Mack. And Eliot.'

I hear her mind working, as though she can make a decision based on this information.

'Don't do any housework, Oleen, while I'm gone,' my mother says. 'I pay someone to do that.'

'Let me know if you see any movie stars,' I call out as she steps off the boat, swinging her purse.

With my mind's eye I follow her as she clatters in her hard sandals over the docks and disappears among the silent motor yachts. I can feel the heat reflected onto her from the wooden boards, and know that at any moment she will need to adjust her scarf. Although she's wearing sunglasses, her eyes will be blinded by the landscape. She won't be able to see the shore, not even the tops of trees. It's all hot blue sky and pushy cut-out images of fibreglass and plexiglas, canvas and nylon flags. On days like this the scene begins to change, her perspective weakens. Boats nearby recede, those in the distance move in. She slips her fingers up under her sunglasses and rubs her eyes.

She locates her BMW in the parking lot, nods to the attendant, turns the air-conditioning to max. My mother will make it a fast trip from Montauk Point to East Hampton, driving twenty miles an hour above the speed limit every inch of the way for a kiddie cone and postcard.

A salty breeze travels through East Hampton, reminding her what little distance she has put between herself and the sea. She steps inside a small shop and scans a rack of postcards. She finds a nice one for her own mother, a bird of some sort on a nest in the sand.

But after she pays for it she hesitates at the counter, wondering whether a shot of historic homes would have been a better choice. Someone behind her clears his throat and she makes a slow and deliberate, haughty turn. An attractive man, with a sunburned nose and cross expression. He doesn't make eye contact with her but it's clear he wants her to move out of his way so he can purchase his Crest and Noxzema.

'I saw Richard Gere,' she tells me. 'You don't believe me. Do you?'

'Mom.'

'Do you?'

I laugh. 'Well, Mom, you do see a lot of that Hollywood crowd.'

She laughs with me. 'I'm just lucky and everyone else is jealous. You haven't been doing any cleaning, now, have you?'

When my mother returns that evening from her rounds of socializing aboard several neighbouring boats, she looks at me hard, then kicks off her shoes and begins stripping off her jewellery.

I ask, 'What is it?'

'Do you really care?' She's having trouble getting her silver bracelets over her wrist. I want to tell her, Try one at a time, but she's borderline right now. She has most of them off when she gives up. She's ready to fling those bracelets across the galley.

'Yes. Really. I care, Mom. Tell me.'

'Okay. Kimberly's husband can't come out this weekend. You know what that means. She'll be over here. And you know how I don't like Kimberly and your father sitting around together all weekend. I end up waiting on the two of them and he starts picking on me.'

'But you and Kimberly are friends,' I say, my back to her now as I begin straightening out the dish towels crammed into one of the drawers.

'Of course we are. Best friends.'

'What did you decide about my friends?'

'Eliot and Mack?'

'Yes.'

'You're not sleeping with both of them, are you?'

I look at her. Her right eye is not quite keeping time with her left. I figure four glasses of wine. I begin slipping on a pair of rubber gloves, but she could never see what was staring her straight in the face after a few drinks.

'No, Mom, only one at a time.'

'Okay, Oleen,' she says wearily. 'Just watch it. I'm going to bed.'

'Already? You only get about thirteen hours of sleep a night.'

'Is it hurting you?' she asks, suddenly nasty.

'No, it isn't hurting me. It's just a lot of sleep.'

'Perhaps some day you'll find, Oleen, that sleep is not so easy to come by. You take it when you can. Besides, nobody asked you here to chart my circadian rhythms.'

But then, nobody asked me here at all.

When she gets up the next morning she's still feeling mean. Even after her coffee she won't speak to me, though when I come out wearing a new bathing suit she can't keep her mouth shut. 'A little modesty wouldn't hurt, Oleen. No one's got the perfect body.' She's wearing a pink wrapper. The hem takes a straight course through the centre of her knees.

But I refuse to change or put on a T-shirt. I locate the sponge and detergent and other cleansers where she hid them behind the gourmet pancake mixes shortly after I arrived.

She dumps her coffee cup in the sink, finds a yoghurt and eats half of it, then casts the spoon and container onto the counter, smearing the dark Arborite with white yoghurt. She folds her arms across her chest and begins taking little steps around the galley.

I scour everything: the white face of the refrigerator, the burners of the Jenn Air range, the faucets and sink. We both get so angry I imagine I can hear the silence struggling with our clenched mouths. After a while we're aware of Kimberly, up above, yoo-hooing.

'There's your best friend,' I say, bending over the sink to scrape vigorously at a chunk of food matter stuck to the faucet.

'What's that supposed to mean?' she snaps.

My father arrives just before noon, within minutes of Eliot and Mack, and is predictably annoyed to find guests on board. But my mother hands him a beer and a bag of pretzels and says, 'Just sit down, Nick. You've had a hard week.' He settles among the deck cushions, out of the direct sun, and begins rolling up his sleeves with a performance so meticulous that by the time he's finished, he's come around.

'Hey, glamour puss,' he says to me. 'New suit?'

But I ignore him, as well as my guests, and watch my mother, because there is a certain pattern we follow, as regular as the movement of a rocking boat. She's fussing about, still in bare feet, straightening cushions and arbitrarily offering cold drinks, her legs silky and brown against her white shorts.

At last she turns and winks at me and together we grin. We both know Dad hasn't had a hard week in years.

When I introduce her to Eliot and Mack, Eliot shakes her hand with that formal, lawyer-like manner he sometimes adopts, while Mack eyes her openly from head to toe. She is pleased to discover they are brothers, as though this can somehow make my relationship with them more respectable. But it's not until you want one and not the other that you understand the mistake you made by sleeping with both.

'You all set for tomorrow night, Jenny?' my father asks my mother. He has removed his socks and shoes and shoved them out into the sun. He begins turning up his pant legs, as though he has made plans to go wading the rest of us know nothing of.

My mother halts in front of him. She takes hold of her blue jersey at the hem, stretching it to her hips then smoothing the cloth flat and neat over her stomach. 'You mean the reunion?' she asks naively.

'We'll have to leave early enough to find a decent motel, somewhere in the vicinity of Stokesley I hope to God, nap and shower and be there by seven-thirty.'

'To tell you the truth, Nick,' she says, taking a seat opposite him and crossing her legs, 'I'm really not interested.'

'What are you saying? I need you to do the driving.'

'Couldn't you find a plane?'

'How's the car?' my father asks me. 'Still getting good mileage?'

'Yeah.'

'They say a tune-up once a year is plenty, but I don't know, sweetheart, with a car like that, I'd bring her in for two. You'll forget half the time and come out even. I'll come out even too, since I paid for her. Twice a year.'

'Yeah, Dad. You told me.' I'm aware of Eliot's amusement. I rise and start for the empty glasses, but my mother shoots me a look and I return to my seat.

'Oleen here thinks she's wise to all matters,' my father says cheerfully. Then he snaps his fingers and says, 'Okay! We'll have lobsters for lunch,' as though someone has just spoken of hunger. His knees have fallen away from each other and one hand has slid into his crotch, loosely holding the can of beer. He nods at Mack and Eliot. He's getting used to them. 'Bit of driving involved with that. After I get another beer – Jenny?

– we'll get organized. Who's coming? We all can't. Where's Kimberly?'

'Lobsters. What a pain in the neck,' Kimberly says. 'This was Nick's idea, wasn't it? Butter ready, Jenny?'

'Microwave,' my mother answers. She prods the pot of heating water with a dish towel wadded in her fist.

'Are those men friends of yours, Oleen?' Kimberly asks me. She's wearing a garish red Oxford shirt so recently removed from its packaging I can see the dark little holes where the pins were slid out.

My father sticks his head below and shouts, though we are less than five feet away. 'Jenny. Did you pack cool clothes? What about my green blazer? Too heavy? Supposed to get into the high nineties tomorrow. It's anyone's guess whether they'll have air conditioning. Better bring that cute little travel iron of yours, too.' He grins at Kimberly and says, 'Hello, stranger,' before withdrawing his head.

'Water's boiling,' Kimberly says. 'Careful, Oleen. That's hot. Better let your mother do it.'

'How old do you think I am?' I ask her.

'I just don't want you to burn yourself, honey.'

'Neither of you touch that pot,' my mother orders and I back away. She whacks at the off/on dials with the dish towel. 'It's not safe. Nick wants lobsters, he can cook them himself.'

'Of course he can, Jenny. He's capable.'

'Oleen, I'm asking you for the last time, get away from those dishes.'

I turn to Kimberly, ignoring my mother, and ask, 'How goes the Japanese make-over?'

'Look here, Oleen,' my mother says. 'If I see you use your fingernails to scrape something off that sink again, I'll break something.' Then she glances around the galley and says, 'Okay, that's it.'

'What?'

'Time to pack.'

'Already?'

'You're packing red wine?'

My mother gives us a tense, dazzling smile. 'Would you two prefer white?'

'Where are we going?' Kimberly asks, suddenly following my mother around the galley.

'A little boat ride. Go find some socks to stuff the wineglasses in, Oleen. *My* socks, not yours.'

'I thought you and Dad never took this thing out.'

'Not this hunk of crap. Your father's afraid of it, the big baby. No, the whaler. Where's that picnic basket?'

She finds the basket – large enough to hold supplies for several families – and we fill it with food and wine. Kimberly and I are smiling, but my mother's look is stern and no-nonsense. 'Put a shirt over that suit, Oleen. This minute! Those men have been ogling you since they arrived.'

When we emerge above deck my father, Mack and Eliot are laughing. My father was always one for a dirty joke, though the laughter drops from his face as my mother passes, lugging that ridiculous basket.

'Oh my, that was a good one,' my father says. 'Lobsters ready, ladies?'

My mother ignores him. Kimberly and I follow her into the whaler.

I don't expect the whaler to start and I certainly don't expect my mother to know how to run it, but she not only gets it going, but has the wherewithal to say, 'Better untie her, Oleen,' as though she does this kind of thing every Friday morning without a cloud in the sky or food in her stomach.

'It's an unsafe world,' my mother says, loud enough for the three left behind to hear, just before she accelerates too quickly and Kimberly falls. 'Your father was always in love with another girl, Oleen. Even in high school.'

'Which one?' my father calls after us. Ashamed, I realize that he honestly wants to know, that it is just this anticipation driving his interest in their high school reunion.

As we move off across the water I watch Eliot and Mack, standing one on either side of my father. Mack laughs, putting an arm around my father, while Eliot gives me that playful, raised-eyebrow look.

Kimberly gets up off the floor of the boat and sits beside me. Her face is screwed up and I think it's because of the fall she's just taken. But she says, 'That bastard! Jenny, even in high school?'

'Listen, Kimberly,' my mother says, turning to examine the two of us with such naked disapproval that I immediately regret getting into the boat with her. 'I think we both know a reliable man is not a husband.'

We run out of gas half an hour later and though we've no idea where we are, Block Island Sound is no wilderness and my mother has kept the boat close to shore. The engine dies off a small strip of white beach.

'Private?' Kimberly asks as we finish the first bottle, our backs stubbornly to the shore.

'Semi-private,' my mother says, glancing over her shoulder. 'Looks like three families.'

'I see four,' Kimberly says.

'Unfortunately, we'll have to get gas from them at some point.'

'What?' I say.

My mother looks at me and kicks the empty gas can.

'People don't bring gasoline with them to the beach, Mom.'

'Well, they'll just have to go home and get some.' She stands and makes her way to the picnic basket at the stern of the boat. She drags the basket back with her, then stumbles returning to her seat. She squeezes in between Kimberly and me, and whispers, 'Did they see that?'

'Yes.'

'Not all of them, Oleen,' Kimberly says.

'I can't believe he expects me to drive all that way to Stokesley tomorrow.' My mother plucks a second bottle of wine from the basket. 'Oleen, you're cut off. You're going to have to do the talking.'

'What?'

'Hush.'

'Why me?'

'Look at Kimberly sitting there with that silly grin and wine all over her shirt.'

'Look at you,' Kimberly says.

'That?' My mother looks down and takes a swipe at her chest. 'That was before we ran out of gas.'

'Mom, don't make me ask them. Can't we come up with a better plan?'

'Stop being so clingy, Oleen. From day one, you couldn't do anything without a hug first.'

I watch her, the concentration on her face making her look young and inexperienced as she uncorks the wine and pours out two glasses without spilling a drop. My eyes begin to sting from the glare on the water and the effort it takes not to blink. My mother and Kimberly are halfway through the second bottle before they realize it's been a while since I've spoken.

'So, Oleen,' Kimberly says. 'They seem like nice men we left back there with Nick. Is one a boyfriend?'

'All right, Oleen,' my mother says, allowing me half a glass. She watches, without comment, as I drain it in one swallow. 'I truly can't remember if you were clingy or not,' she lies, 'I was so exhausted.' Suddenly her voice turns soft, almost tender. 'But you know what you used to say at bedtime, don't you? You used to hold my face in your hands, and say, "You're the best mommy in the universe."'

'The older one? Mack? Is that his name? About how old is he, Oleen?'

'You were four or five. You said that to me every night before you fell asleep.'

'Look, Jenny,' Kimberly says. 'I don't see how you can let Oleen here go around with that man. Mack? He must be thirty-five.'

My mother frowns. She wants Kimberly to drop it. She wants us to savour the image of me holding her face, cherishing her, reading her mind.

But sometimes reading your mother's mind can be hard going.

'What about this?' I say. 'Daddy's locked himself in his study and you spend an entire evening kicking the door.'

My mother looks at me like I've gone mad.

'Only joking, Mom.'

'Some joke.' My mother leans into Kimberly and says conspiratorially, 'Remember what terrible PMS I had back then?'

'You're in the kitchen sweeping everything in the cupboards onto the floor.' I put my hand over my mouth.

'That'll do, Oleen. Not another sip for you, princess.'

'PMS,' Kimberly says, peering over the edge of the boat as though she is trying to discover what she remembers of it at the bottom of the sea.

'You bet,' my mother says. 'It ravaged me.'

'I've never had PMS in my life,' I say.

'You don't get it until you've had children,' my mother lectures. She shifts on the bench so that we are no longer touching at the shoulders. 'It takes over your life. It's a week getting it, a week getting clear of it, then two weeks free and all over again.'

Kimberly sits up straight as a pencil. 'I hate to say this, Jenny, but you sound just like my daughters. They're always coming out with something cruel, storming out of the house, then calling later to say, sorry

Mom, it's just P M S, or ovulation, or post-partum depression.'

She pauses, taking a minute to stand and then another to stay standing, balancing herself with legs spread. She's wearing yellow shorts, much shorter than my mother wears hers. My mother and I immediately examine the fat around her knees.

Kimberly raises a finger. 'But you know what I want to know?'

I glance over at the beach and see that we have a good audience, children included. A toy poodle is stepping in and out of the waves, barking at us. We're close to hitting bottom.

'I want to know what the heck did we do?' Kimberly cries. 'What did we do, Jenny, when the kids were messing up the house and the hormones were running through our bodies and our husbands were coming in the door expecting a candlelit dinner? We didn't go whining on and on about P M S.'

'Mom threw Daddy's suits around the house. Bowls of cereal down the hall. Books and magazines into the shower.'

'She's exaggerating,' my mother says, refusing to look at me.

'Of course she is. We all do.'

'You don't know anything about it,' my mother says to me. 'But quite frankly, Kimberly, I don't recall any candlelit dinners.

'Sit down, Kimberly,' she adds. 'You're rocking the boat.'

'So?' Kimberly asks me. 'Mack? Eliot? Which one?'

'Both of them,' my mother says. 'My daughter's a slut.'

'You give me a glass of wine, I'll tell you.'

They both offer me theirs. I take my mother's but she's quick to pour another.

'Eliot,' I answer, with a wistful wine-heavy sigh. 'But apparently I suffocate him.'

'Not Mack?' Kimberly asks.

'Nah.'

'I thought Mack had a lot of animal magnetism,' Kimberly confides.

My mother bursts out laughing. She wipes her mouth with her palm. 'That's precious. What the hell do you know about animal magnetism, Kimberly?'

But before Kimberly can defend herself our eyes meet, and I give her a look that lets her know my mother is not just throwing words to the wind.

'Eliot said that?' my mother demands. This has made her angry. 'That you suffocate him?'

I nod. 'He's not into monogamy. Too clingy.'

My mother's face changes and she asks, 'Are you forgetting that sometimes we were happy?'

'You were always breaking things, Mom,' I insist. But the resentment has left me. From a distance now I see us: she is dropping a carton of milk or bag of rice and I am rushing over with a cloth or broom.

'It was exhausting,' I say. 'The worrying I did.'

My mother's eyes are watery, but her voice is her own. 'Have you finished?'

'Just forget about me,' Kimberly says. She has managed to find a comb in the picnic basket and is ripping it through her hair. 'I've seen plenty. Life is not a pretty picture.'

'Of course it isn't. To this very day I'm still dropping things. Clumsiness is one of the symptoms. PMS is this, Oleen, it's being one step behind the rest of the world.' She snatches the wineglass from my hand. 'And, as your father should know by now, I find driving the car utterly nerve-racking.'

Our backs are to the shore. When the boat hits, the three of us turn in unison. A handsome wet man is standing in the water with his hand on the bow of our boat. He studies us, taking in the empty bottles, uneaten food, our drained faces. For a moment he looks frightened, then smiles politely and says, 'You ladies look like you could use a hand getting this back up and running.'

'Yes, we could,' my mother explains graciously. 'What we need is a drop of gasoline.'

As soon as he turns away, my mother puts her face into mine. 'You know that man resembled Alec Baldwin one heck of a lot, Oleen. You thought that, too, didn't you?'

'I'll have to have a better look when he swims back out with the gas, Mom. Why don't you ask him?'

'I just might, princess. I just might.'

We're all smiling now. I bend to tidy the mess at our feet, relieved that gas is on its way, that soon we will be putting this boat ride behind us.

WINSTON

THE BOY IS WALKING in a lopsided circle on the restaurant's deck, encompassing one empty table and a trolley of dirty plates, glasses and napkins. He eyes the tips of his ripped sneakers as they advance beneath him – sneakers that Fritz has struggled long and hard to replace. But Fritz, whose hair is blond and thinning and whose voice can be as tender as an angel's, is someone the boy is still learning to love.

He collides with the trolley and it rattles. A balled napkin drops silently to the floor.

'Winston,' Eleanor calls. 'Come back in here with us.'

He stops and looks at his mother, reluctant to go back inside the restaurant where she sits with those two men.

'Now I grant you,' Barry is saying. He is a large man and easily fills the space between the two tables. 'Mother had it forever. When we were boys she told us time and time again: Tiger was her oldest – her dearest – friend.'

Eleanor has known Fritz's brother, Barry, less than an hour, yet already he is into a third story about his mother, this time telling it to two expensively dressed women who have abandoned their lunch and turned, spellbound, to listen to him. They are sitting at an adjacent table set for four, stealing looks at Eleanor.

'Winston,' she calls again.

'Leave the boy,' Barry tells her. 'Where did my brother go?'

'He's paying.'

'Right. Old money-bags. I was twelve when the cat died,' he continues, returning to the two women. 'And sure enough, Mother had the thing stuffed.'

'You're kidding me!' one of the women blurts out, then immediately covers her mouth with a hand and blushes.

'I am not,' Barry says. 'Cost Father a good five hundred. And wasn't it a horror to look at. When Mother put it in her lap, we all left the room.' Barry stops and sits back with a troubled faraway look, as though this walk down memory lane is beginning to drain him. He looks out again at Winston. 'I wonder what that boy of yours is thinking.'

But Eleanor ignores Barry. As though her coolness serves to revive him, he suddenly pounds the table where the two women are sitting, his expression now wide awake and fresh. The women slowly draw their hands off the table and into their laps. 'Well, ladies,' he says. 'I just hope for Mother's sake she's put that old cat away and is getting on with life. I'm all for life.'

The two women nod, glancing uneasily at each other. Something isn't quite right about this man, they are at last deciding.

But he has swung away from them, giving them his back. He makes an effort to smile at Eleanor.

'I should warn you,' he says. 'There's a rat on board. An eternal problem on boats.'

He sees that she is quick to cover her alarm. Her skin has an ugly pink cast and her eyes are glassy. She looks haggard; he wonders how well she sleeps.

'Ah,' he says, with mock relief. 'Here he is: my brother.'

Fritz sits down beside Eleanor. Barry watches him touch her, solemnly, on her knee. 'So. Where is he?' Fritz asks.

She gestures towards Winston wandering around the deck.

'Leave him, he's fine,' Barry orders, impatient now. 'I know. I've been here a hundred times. They like kids here. Bar Harbor. It's a family place.'

They leave the restaurant and wander through Main Street, moving towards the town marina where Barry's sailboat is tied on. As Eleanor descends the ramp to the boats, Fritz shouts, 'Eleanor, aren't you watching him?'

Fritz scurries down the ramp, passing her, and grabs Winston who is tiptoeing along the edge of the floating dock. 'Gotta be careful, Winston. Gotta start using our heads if we wanna be sailors,' he says softly.

Barry wakes them early the next morning and ushers them above deck for sunrise. He hauls up a large bag of oranges and Winston follows, grinning, with a box of doughnuts. Eleanor and Fritz sit side by side, yawning. The boat is anchored off a small fishing village edged with black, spear-shaped trees. Eleanor stares blankly at the cotton balls of fog separating from the rock shore.

'I'm going to catch a shark, Mommy,' Winston tells his mother shyly. He steps across the deck cushions to get closer to her. 'Barry said so. Watch out. It might bite my head off.'

'A shark? Can you eat a shark?' Eleanor asks sleepily.

'I won't eat it,' he says, laughing, a little proud of his mother's silliness. 'It'll be my pet.'

'Just pretend?'

'No!'

'Sand sharks,' Barry explains. 'Harmless.'

'There's the sun,' Fritz says. 'What a morning.'

'Winston doesn't understand,' Eleanor tells Barry.

'Yes, I do,' the boy whispers, embarrassed.

'What about this rat?' Fritz asks.

The boy is sitting across from Fritz and his mother with the sun at his back, enjoying the warmth he feels on his shoulders and head. He watches the sunlight hit his mother's short brown hair and that little puff on top from sleeping on her back. Beside her, Fritz's sparse blond hair is shining like gold thread over his red scalp.

'What rat?' Winston says.

'Just a rat,' Barry says. 'Leave it alone.'

'Well, I don't know.' Fritz looks at Eleanor.

The boy looks at his mother.

'Eleanor?' Fritz says. 'Are you listening? What do you think?'

'I'm completely neutral about it,' she says eventually. She is staring at the water. She hasn't made eye contact with anyone in a while and the boy is beginning to worry that something is wrong.

'So we'll trap it,' Fritz tells his brother. 'Get rid of it for you.'

'It's a rodent, not a monster,' Barry says. 'It's been on board for months. My vote is we leave it. But you're the guests.'

'What do you think, Eleanor?' Fritz asks. 'Trap it?'

Eleanor tries to look at Barry but the sun must be in her face; the boy watches as she squints and her face scrunches up. 'Why are you asking *me?*'

'You could always poison it,' Barry says, though even the boy knows he doesn't mean this.

Fritz sighs. 'He's just a boy.'

Winston looks at his mother. Anything that frightens him usually frightens her. But she may not be listening and he doesn't want any trouble.

'I want the rat,' he says with force.

Fritz smiles and pats Winston on the head. 'Is there a trap, Barry?'

'No.'

'A project. Well, all right,' Fritz says.

Barry nods, scowling at a small outboard passing only a few feet away. Two boys and a girl are standing in it, their mouths open, laughing. As the sailboat rolls in the wake of the outboard, the boy stumbles against his mother. 'Mommy. I'm going to catch a rat. It's going to be my pet.'

Eleanor's eyes retreat from the water. She puts her hand firmly around Winston's wrist.

'You don't understand.'

'Don't change anything, Mommy.'

'What will we use for bait?' Fritz asks.

'Hot dogs,' the boy cries, and they all laugh.

Once evening comes, Fritz begins. On the narrow table below deck he sets out wire, electrical tape, pliers, an empty juice can. Barry and Eleanor sit across from each other, observing Fritz.

Winston is standing, leaning first on Barry, then on Fritz, holding the hot dog. Each time he glances at his mother he grows more unsettled. He experiences, though without recognizing it, what she experiences: the nagging, uncomfortable feeling of being packed in too closely.

'When I catch the rat —' he begins.

'Easy. Take it easy, Winston,' Fritz says. 'If you keep knocking against me I won't get this perfect.'

'When I catch the rat,' Winston says quietly, 'it might bite me.'

'Take it easy, I said. Go over and sit with your mother.'

Instead, Winston allows Barry to lift him onto his lap. 'It might,' he insists, casting an angry look first at Fritz, then at his silent mother.

'Hey! Feel this boy's heart beat.' Barry's hand is fanned monstrously over Winston's chest. He removes it and replaces it with one of Winston's, a fourth the size of his own. 'Feel that?' Barry says. 'It's pumping a mile a minute.'

Winston concentrates hard. There is something caught inside his body. 'What is it?'

'Your heart,' Barry says. 'A machine. I have one, too. You don't know about your own heart? What did you think was in there? Stuffing?' He looks at Eleanor. 'Don't you teach him anything?'

Eleanor shifts in her seat as though she might be getting ready to go above deck, but then settles back into her seat. 'Do I look like an expert on human anatomy?'

'No. Not particularly. It's just a machine that pushes your blood around,' Barry tells Winston, moving his forearm up and down like a piston. 'Pump, pump. Your mother has one, too. Go feel hers.'

Winston looks across at his mother but her expression is guarded. He decides that he isn't interested in putting his hand anywhere on her at this moment.

'There we go,' Fritz says, lifting the trap. 'Where should I put it?'

Winston stands and begins to pace around the cramped galley. 'Mommy.'

'Yes.'

Winston stops. 'Mommy, look at me.'

'I am.'

He starts pacing again. 'I need to buy a machine what makes string. Can you buy me that?'

'Yeah, all right.'

Winston frowns. 'Listen to me, Mommy.'

'I am.'

'Put it under the sink, next to the garbage,' Barry says to Fritz.

'I need a machine what makes string. Long, long string to put around the rat's mouth so he won't bite us.'

'The rat isn't that big,' Barry says. 'Look, it's going to fit inside that can.'

Winston ignores the can. 'I'm going to make a humongous knot.'

Fritz pauses, holding the trap. 'Eleanor,' he says. 'I think it's bedtime.'

'No! I need that machine.'

'We shouldn't have to put up with this,' Fritz reminds Eleanor.

Eleanor rises heavily and approaches Winston.

The boy looks at his mother and then at Fritz. 'No! I am not going to do what you mean,' he yells, throwing himself down. 'I AM GOING TO WRAP THE STRING AROUND YOUR MOUTH!'

'Winston,' Barry says calmly. 'The boat's full of machines.'

'Do you have a machine what makes string?'

'I've got plenty of string. Rope too.'

'Long, long string?'

'We shouldn't have to bribe him,' Eleanor hears Fritz say as she half lifts, half drags Winston into the forward cabin.

He falls asleep immediately. Eleanor pushes on the hatch above her and rises waist-high into the night and lights a joint. She hears the cold slosh of the ocean against the sides of the boat and sees the amber anchor light hanging high above her. She thinks of Winston's face overwhelmed and pinched into anger, and Fritz's, expecting results.

She slips back down and cautiously closes the hatch overhead. She leans across Winston and kisses his cheek. He smells of raw hot dog.

'Didn't you hear me?' Fritz is asking. He's only a few feet away, looking at her suspiciously. 'I've been calling you. Come back out and be sociable.'

'Do I have to? I'd rather chew nails.' But she is smiling.

'Yes, you have to,' he says, smiling too.

He leads her by the hand, though the moment she is back out she knows it was a mistake.

'Don't worry,' Barry says as she sits opposite him. 'He's a great kid. Kids are kids.'

'Kids need rules,' Fritz says from under the sink where he is installing the trap.

Barry lifts the pliers and leans across the table, his body covering it. He says to her, 'Listen to this. Once I took a metal spoon and placed it on a hot burner. Give me your hand.'

Eleanor glances across at Fritz who has stopped to watch, grinning. 'He's not going to hurt you,' he assures her.

'Give me your hand.'

Eleanor puts her hand out and Barry picks it up as though it could be anything: a dish, a rag, a piece of paper. 'When the spoon was red-hot I called for my brother.' Barry sinks the pliers into Eleanor's palm. 'Then I put the spoon in his hand.'

'Fritz?'

'He's my only brother.' Barry releases her hand. 'But I was just a kid. These are the things kids do.'

Eleanor slides her hand off the table and into her lap. Fritz is giving her a timid smile; he's hoping she'll feel sorry for him. As soon as she realizes this, she feels fine.

'What did your mother do?' she asks, not caring at all.

'That's another story,' Barry says, scrutinizing her.

'He bribed me not to tattle,' Fritz explains. 'He paid me.'

'Mother was out to lunch, even then,' Barry says matter-of-factly. 'You're stoned, aren't you?'

'Shit, Eleanor. You promised.'

'Holding out on us?'

'Don't encourage her, Barry.'

'When? When did I promise?' she says, fed up with both of them, with their mother and her dead cat. With this desire of theirs that she share their past.

She rises and returns to her cabin but Fritz is right behind her. She quickly stretches out so that her head touches Winston's in the crook of the V-berth and there isn't space for another body.

'Would you like me to rub your neck?' Fritz asks.

'No.'

'Rub mine?'

'No.'

'Can I get in?'

'No.'

'There are some issues, Eleanor, we should start addressing.'

She knows he's trying hard to sound kind, reasonable. She eyes him from a safe distance and asks, 'Like what?'

They anchor off a small deserted island ringed with slabs of creamy granite. The middle of the island is nothing more than a few short pines and bayberry in a tousled field. Eleanor and Winston cut across it, startling yellow and orange warblers from trees before coming upon an abandoned house on the far side.

The house is small and empty – a single floor, a single room. Both inside and out it is weather-worn and grey. A granite block rests at the doorstep and on either side beach plums bloom higher than the windows, almost higher than the house. Brown sand reaches up from the water.

Winston wanders into the house. Eleanor sits in the doorway and waits for him.

Eventually he comes out and sits beside her, though he would prefer to crawl into her lap. From this elevation the ocean looks narrow and powerless. He hasn't felt like himself in a long time, but he doesn't really know this. He beats his feet rhythmically on the hard sand until it begins seeping in through the holes at the tips of his sneakers.

He can't get that pumping out of his mind. 'I'm gonna make a machine what counts blood,' he tells his mother.

'Are you,' she says, but she isn't listening.

By the time they return to the boat the weather has turned hot and still. As they eat lunch in the cockpit, Winston describes the abandoned house.

'Why didn't you wait for me?' Fritz says to Eleanor.

'You wanted to come? I didn't know.'

'You knew.' He knocks over his beer and opens another. Barry bends down and wipes the spill with someone's shirt.

'This house, Winston. Anything in it?' Barry asks.

'No. It was just right.'

Fritz says, 'You're not telling me you went in?'

'Mommy said I could.'

'They're calling for bad weather,' Barry says, yawning.

'You let him in an old shack, Eleanor?' Fritz says. 'It could have collapsed. What were you thinking? That wouldn't be very pleasant, Winston, I can assure you.'

The boy freezes, thinking of the pretty house collapsing on itself without a sound. He wants to say to Fritz, 'Don't scare me.' Then he sees Barry throw his egg salad sandwich overboard and is somehow consoled.

'They're calling for bad weather,' Barry repeats.

'All right. We heard you the first time,' Fritz says.

The boy steps down. 'What?'

'We've got to find a harbour somewhere, Winston, that's all, no big deal,' Fritz says. 'Because it might get really windy and off we'd go, blown away.'

'Shut up, Fritz,' Eleanor says.

Winston immediately begins circling the well of the cockpit, around and around. His mother lifts her legs to give him room.

'Mommy.' He stops and reaches a hand up to her face. 'Look at me.'

'I am.'

'When the wind comes …' He starts to pace again. 'Mommy!'

'I am.'

'When the wind comes it's going to take the roof off the boat.'

'Take it easy, Winston,' Fritz says. 'Jesus.'

'Yes. I saw it in a nightmirror.'

'Nightmare,' Fritz says.

'Nightmare!'

'Winston,' Barry says. 'By morning the storm will be over.'

'By morning the roof will be gone,' the boy says.

'No, Winston,' his mother says. 'Just stop talking to him, Barry.'

Fritz leans over to touch Eleanor and Winston is halted by his out-stretched arm. 'Just one thing, Eleanor. Where were you last week?'

Barry stands.

'Have you stopped answering your phone or something?'

'Eleanor!'

They all look up at Barry.

'Get a life jacket for Winston. Time to pull anchor.'

Eleanor goes below and looks around in the sudden dark for a life jacket. When she doesn't immediately see one, she gives up. The galley smells of polished wood and egg salad. As she lights a joint she briefly wonders where the rat is hiding.

She wakes much later. She has been asleep on her stomach in the V-berth. She feels the boat gently heave itself against something and produce a creaking moan. They must be docking. She pushes on the hatch above and drags herself up onto the deck. The first thing she sees is the shore, where white houses with black shutters sit like boxes among the dark exploding trees.

Rope hits the deck behind her and she turns. Barry is securing the boat and Winston is standing beside him in his life jacket, eyeing her in that careful way of his. She rises, feeling collapsed and negligible and hating it; her clothing sticks to her body and she stumbles, as though the boat is still chopping into waves beneath them.

'Look, Mommy,' Winston says.

A yellow sailboat is approaching, gliding like a skater, its crew searching for a place to dock. The sails are down and the engine on, just a hum. Suddenly the women on board begin waving. It takes Eleanor a moment to realize they are the two from the restaurant. She turns to Barry, but though he paid them such hungry, gracious attention only days earlier, he ignores them now and Eleanor finds herself compelled to wave. She smiles feebly.

Barry yanks his shirt over his head and tosses it down with the manner of someone fed up with everyone, including himself. Just before leaping into the sea he glances back at Eleanor, whose waving hand drops. The splash comes up and hits her legs like cold coins.

The moment Barry disappears beneath the water, the boy's panic sets in. He begins waving frantically at the yellow sailboat, although he has never seen these people before in his life and soon both they and his mother, who has turned to go below deck, are gone. Barry swims a while then climbs back into the boat, the smell of the ocean a bubble around him, and goes below, too.

The boy remains above, even after the first drops of rain splatter the deck, and returns the ends of the ropes to their tidy coils, which he knows that Barry, had he not gone swimming, would have remembered to do.

By evening, the storm hits. Sea water slashes the small windows and the boat repeatedly punches the dock. Barry sits at the chart table flipping through his handbooks with his back to everyone.

The boy's first thought when he hears the noise is that the wind has broken something and now they will surely die. But the next moment the door beneath the sink pops opens and the juice can rolls out and lodges against Barry's stool.

'We got him!' Fritz cries. He bends for the can, lifts the trap door he worked so hard to perfect, and peers in. 'Christ.' He looks at his brother. 'It's a mouse.'

Barry shrugs as though he knew this all along. 'I told you, I never minded it.'

The boy stands slowly in his seat. He puts a hand on his mother's shoulder to protect her.

'Winston,' Fritz says. 'Come look.'

But the boy shakes his head.

'Get rid of it,' Barry says, as though discussing a plate of leftovers. The boy can't see his face. Only his rounded shoulders and head bent once again over his charts.

Fritz, who seems angry, puts a foot on the companionway. 'Toss it overboard?' he asks Barry.

'Whatever suits you.'

'No!' The boy scrambles out of his seat and Eleanor rises behind him. Barry turns on his stool with mild curiosity, then slouches back, his hands falling open as though he doesn't hold out much hope for these people.

'You had your chance, Winston,' Fritz says. 'I've tried to involve you – with everything. From day one I have.'

'But it's my pet, remember?' the boy pleads. 'A shark might come up and bite it.'

'Christ. Not everything in the world is going to come up and bite everything else,' Fritz says, shaking the can so that the animal inside can be heard thumping from side to side.

The boy looks at his mother. Sometimes she can be so slow it drives him crazy.

'The mouse is going over the side,' Fritz says. 'Period.' But he doesn't move.

It's a test, the boy decides. 'I don't love him,' he whispers to his mother. He's desperate.

She sighs. She looks so tired. 'Jesus, Fritz, can I have that can?'

'It's my pet,' the boy tries to explain, hoping Fritz understands how simple this is: a simple exchange of one plan for another.

'Over the side and into the ocean. Period.'

Eleanor puts her hand out. 'Listen to yourself, Fritz. It's just a mouse. Give it to me.'

Fritz stares at Eleanor, and the boy recognizes his luck in not being left alone with him just now. He steps closer to his mother.

Fritz shoves the can at Eleanor, pushing it hard against her belly, and she flinches. For a moment she stands there, confused, holding the can away from herself; Winston begins to worry she'll drop it, but suddenly she turns to him and he takes it.

'I need a safe place for this,' he says.

Barry rises at once and begins clearing a spot on a shelf for the can. As he and Winston surround it with books to prevent it from rolling around in the night, the boy twice glances over his shoulder at Fritz with a look of trepidation, but also of warning.

'Safe and sound,' Barry says.

'Tomorrow someone will need to buy me a cage,' Winston announces with confidence, despite the quick look of hatred Fritz directs toward him. But the boy is more himself now and has the odd but not entirely unfamiliar suspicion that his desires are connected to these three adults by some very strong string.

'It's just a mouse,' Fritz says. 'It's not even a rat.'

You're too late, Winston thinks, allowing himself to feel sorry for Fritz now. It's when they start to sound stupid that the boy knows they're finished.

GLADSTONE, 1957

STANLEY ARRIVED HOME just as his wife was starting on the kitchen floor. Somehow she'd moved all the chairs outside to stand in the shadow of the hemlocks and pushed the kitchen table up against a wall. Now she was kneeling on the floor, a cushion beneath her knees, and he watched as she travelled steadily away from him, sliding the cushion with her folded legs, dragging the bucket alongside her.

'Floor looks nice, Marigold. What's Nana doing back there?'

'Tying the porch door shut.'

'They have some nifty mops for the floor now, dear. Sponge on the end? You squeeze out the dirty water with a metal handle.' He paused, wanting her to understand how brilliant they were, wanting her to stop and ask him to go on. 'Whole rack of them over at the hardware store in Centerville,' he said. 'Squeeze-action sponge mops.'

But Marigold did not seem to have heard. She paused, her hands on her knees, the cloth sopping in a puddle on the floor, and said, 'She's driving me crazy. Leaving food out for dead people. Inviting all manner of ants. Daddy's not hungry, or thirsty. He's dead in the ground.'

Stanley had nothing to say to this. He stood outside the door, barred by the wet floor, the small overnight bag still in his hand and suit jacket over his arm, reluctant to turn and take them up the steps to the sleeping cottage behind him. He stared at the frayed sunlight falling through the trees and screened windows and onto his wife at the end of an empty floor, claiming the top of her head, the skirt smooth on her lap, the white rubber soles of her shoes.

Nana turned away from securing the door. Trapped by her approaching daughter and the bucket, she began to hobble from one foot to the other like a jittery pony. She glanced outside at Stanley and her lips pursed over her old teeth. All day, he knew, she watched his two daughters run in one door and out another. 'They should be going out the way they come in, Stanley,' she called to him now. "Specially the baby. Her luck will change.'

'Ma, she's seven years old,' Marigold said without looking up.

'Neither one's a baby any more.'

'Looks no more'n four.'

'Ma.'

'Those mops, dear?' Stanley asked his wife again. He was begging for the go-ahead to spend money on something it was unlikely she would ever see the beauty of. 'Shall I run out and get you one? They're in at the hardware store.'

Marigold lifted the cloth from the bucket and bent over the floor. She scrubbed furiously. 'And how do you suppose I'm going to manage a gadget like that with two crutches in tow?'

Stanley looked through the screens into the living room where one of her crutches was propped against a table. She'd owned these crutches so long now, the same she'd brought home from the hospital. They had a smell he could conjure up even at this distance, a smell that was there when he closed his eyes at night.

'How are you feeling?' he asked, a wave of affection for her taking him. She washed the floors and swept the screens. She cooked, she cleaned, she wrung out laundry and limped along with a single crutch from tree to tree, clipping clothes to the line. She sat at the kitchen table with her cigarettes and pad of paper and made out lists.

He watched her now as she sat back on her heels and dabbed at her lap with her wet hands, then took a cigarette from her apron pocket. 'My hip hurts, what did you expect? And my armpits, they're very tender in this heat.' She lit the cigarette and exhaled the smoke so that it uncoiled past her face towards the exposed beams of a ceiling never properly finished.

'Do you see my crutch anywhere, Stanley?'

He put his things down and went around the cottage, entering it from the front. He took the crutch where it was leaning against the table in the living room and handed it in through the kitchen to her. Then he went back onto the porch, out of sight, and lay down on the daybed. He felt he should go up to the sleeping cottage and take off his suit, but he was tired from the drive and from carrying around the good news inside him for so long.

He stared up through the limbs of birch and hemlock. The sky was very blue. In the air was the sweet smell of sun heating old wood, and the fishiness that comes from lake water washing back and forth over a rocky shore all day.

* * *

She had fallen down on the ice and broken her hip in March. She'd brought him here, and he had stared at three shabby cottages beside a boot-shaped lake in an empty stretch of western Massachusetts. The nearest town, Gladstone, was only a few miles away, but it was a place that even today he could not fully accept. At the crossing of two country roads, Gladstone then and now offered only two things: a squat brick library and the white Congregational Church where they eventually married.

She had been thirsty. This Stanley recalled as though it were last week, but other things, like her face that day, were lost to him. He followed her away from the cottages and over a small rise into the woods. Rigid skeletal trunks, bushes oddly thick with green leaves, ahead of him her pulsing, darkening fur coat. The frozen ground like concrete. In a clearing she paused and he stepped past her. There was the scent of wet moss and decaying pine needles. She said, *Who's been drawing water here?* Then he slid across the ice. He grabbed the handle of the well pump sheathed in thin ice that crumbled as he caught himself, then turned back just as she lurched towards him. She landed bluntly on her right hip. He picked her up.

* * *

Bobbie was using two hands to carry Mortimer's glass of water as she passed her snoring father on tiptoe. Lydia was close behind.

Nana maintained her husband returned every night out of sheer thirst. 'Just what I need,' she said. 'A dead man pestering me for a drink in the pitch dark.'

Bobbie stopped. Her father's chest rose and fell and his face looked cold and goose-fleshy. When Lydia reached for the glass, Bobbie released it to her without a murmur, then watched as Lydia dunked her fingers into Mortimer's water and began flicking it at their father.

After a few minutes he opened his eyes. 'Hey. What's the big idea?'

He got to his feet. Bobbie fumbled at her sister's arms, tripped over a loose floorboard, backed into a table.

'Did you wake him?' Marigold asked as they ran up behind her, clutching her apron. 'Watch out, girls, that stove is hot. There you are, Stan. Supper's sitting here ready. What's the matter with you?'

'I'm wet ... sticky. Those girls. Is it possible they were spitting on me?'

Bobbie's terror was punishment enough, but he was hungry to whack Lydia, who stood there behind her mother, boldly sticking out her tongue.

'You're too close,' Marigold complained, pushing the girls away and trying to balance, without a crutch, against the stone sink. 'Stop terrorizing them, Stanley.'

'Look, Marigold. I'm soaked.'

'Sweating in your sleep, that's all it was.'

Stanley yanked open the cupboard drawer and the plates on the shelves above rattled. He lifted out a dish towel and patted his face.

'Stanley, not a clean towel!'

He told them the good news at supper. He was sitting at the end of the table. 'It's just what we've been looking for,' he explained. He looked at each of them in turn but none would meet his eye.

'I thought we'd visit first, just for a look. A holiday. Did I tell you I met Roland's wife? Dora? Those women have such a great time.' He looked at the girls. 'Your mother would love a holiday.'

'Over my dead body,' Marigold said.

'Dora said to bring the family.' He glanced at Nana. 'The whole kit 'n' caboodle. I wish we could get your mother on a holiday.' He turned to Bobbie but she looked away. 'It's just what your mother needs.'

'Like heck it is.'

'I was born in Gladstone,' Nana said. 'So was Marigold.'

'The coast is lovely, dear. Great schools, shopping, the works.' Yet he had to admit it was not the sort of excursion for which his wife was well suited.

'I was born here,' Nana repeated.

Later, while Marigold washed the dishes and handed them to Lydia and Bobbie for drying, Stanley stood behind them. 'The baby-blue Atlantic Ocean,' he said. 'You girls could horse around on the beach and make sand castles. Your mother could meet Dora. There's not an ounce of snobbery in that woman, dear. She's opened up their house to us.' He stopped and pressed his foot over a spot where the linoleum was curling away from the wall and would not lie flat. He had not cried since he was five, though he had a sudden memory of how it felt to be driven to it by disappointment.

'The position is no good, Marigold, if we live here, the middle of nowhere. The sticks.'

She was staring out the window. It was possible she hadn't heard a word.

'A good impression if you came with me, dear.'

Then, right out of the clear blue, his wife was turning away from the sink, the rag in her hand dripping water across the toes of her bad leg, saying to him, 'All right, Stan, we'll go. Just for the day.'

He had been driving two and a half hours. The heat in the car was brutal. He could hear Nana, overdressed, rustling around in the back seat where she sat between his daughters and the two crutches.

'How are you, Nana?' he asked, trying to find her in the rear-view mirror.

'I'm burning up.'

Marigold turned. 'Take off some clothes, Ma. Take off that wool sweater. My Lord.'

'I will not,' Nana said.

'Your arms, Nana,' Lydia said. 'I can't look.'

'Study something else,' Nana said, pulling her sleeves down.

'She's got the hives, Stanley,' Marigold said.

Stanley nodded and his heart sank, though so gradually he was not fully aware of it.

Nana leaned forward over the back of the front seat, close to Stanley's shoulder. Her breath was horrible. 'What in damnation is that ahead of us?'

'Boston, Nana,' Stanley said. 'Bet it's some time since you been there?'

'Yoo-hoo, Stanley, I got no interest in that place.'

'Of course not, Nana,' he said quickly, regretting his stupidity.

'We won't be going directly through Boston, will we?' Marigold asked.

'Dear, we are en route.'

'There must be another *en route.*'

'Marigold,' Nana said. 'Did we leave anything out for your father?'

'Will you please sit back, Ma,' Marigold said. 'All of you. It's hot enough. Spread out.'

'Looks like rain over your Boston,' Nana pointed out.

'Boston is dangerous. And filthy,' Marigold said.

'For Chrissakes, I practically live here,' Stanley said. Job hunting, week after week, he'd travelled this way, heading to a place where people were out and about in the world, and now it was paying off. He couldn't ask for a nicer boss than Roland, who, it was Stanley's secret opinion, couldn't ask for a nicer wife than Dora.

'Nana,' Bobbie said gently. 'I wish you would stop scratching yourself. You're only bleeding now.'

It started raining. Suffocating, summer rain.

'Not even a glass of water?' Nana asked her daughter.

Marigold spun around and Stanley felt the air beside him stir. 'For the love of the Lord, Ma, will you forget all that? And take off that wool sweater! Girls, roll up your windows.'

'Forget it,' Lydia said, her voice high, pinched. 'I'm boiling. I'll perish.'

'Hold on,' Stanley said, slowing the car. 'What would you girls say to some cool refreshments?'

'Where are you taking us now, Stanley! Isn't anybody listening to me? Roll up those windows!'

Stanley stopped the car and reached a hand kindly in his wife's direction. 'Marigold. Dear. We're perfectly safe.'

Nana grunted, staring out past the wet glass. 'They'll catch that polio.'

'They're at no risk of polio,' Stanley said, unable, finally, to keep the scorn from his voice. He looked at his daughters and asked, 'Have you had your vaccinations?'

'Stanley,' Marigold said. 'That doctor was an idiot.'

'No surprise there,' said Nana.

Stanley glanced once more at his wife. She looked as though she might have already been out in a light rain. And Nana could use something on those arms.

He made the decision quickly, the way he believed all decisions should be made, allowing no time for dilly-dallying or a change of heart. He waited until the traffic was clear, then took the car out into the road, spun it around and headed home.

'That's better,' Nana said.

'It's cooler already,' Marigold whispered. The relief in her voice made it easier to forgive her.

He drove a long time in the pounding rain, thinking how he would put it to Roland on the phone. Or Dora, if she should answer, which he hoped she would not. How could a woman like Dora understand a woman like Marigold?

After a while he realized they were all asleep. Marigold's head was tipped back. Beneath one eye a thin muscle gently twitched. Behind him, Nana slept upright between the two crutches, Lydia and Bobbie fallen towards her, each of their soft faces braced by the wooden slats of a crutch.

It was stuffy in the car. His was the only window down, but just a crack, because of the rain. He was asleep only seconds, but in those seconds he dreamed he was kneeling on a lake of green ice holding Marigold in his arms. Embedded in the ice around him were pine needles and broken leaves, and far below the surface nearing the floor of the lake there was something else: two crutches, distorted by the ice, but new, never used. When the ice began to crack loudly, like thunder, from shore to shore, he feared he could hold on to her no longer and would lose her. Then the car hit the shoulder and he opened his eyes onto the road.

* * *

Nana was not there that March day when Stanley carried Marigold back from the well. Had she been, she would have been surprised by Stanley's white look of determination and her daughter's lack of composure.

After Marigold had been a week in the hospital, with Stanley driving Nana back and forth to Boston, the surgeon asked to see them. He said Marigold's broken hip was infected. Staphylococcus bacterium, he said, as though he knew what he was talking about. But Nana knew he was a nobody. A doorknob, a bucket of slop.

A week later the infection had spread. The surgeon explained, I need to cut more out.

When Marigold left the hospital her right leg was several inches shorter than her left. The toes on her bad leg, as it would come to be called, just reached the floor. They gave her crutches to use temporarily. Soon, they explained, she'd have no difficulty with a customized orthopedic shoe and the occasional use of a cane.

Nana and Marigold exchanged a look that was between them as clear as water. But Stanley was not privy to it.

In the years following the accident, Nana began to inspect her closets and the corners of her room each evening before bed. She rose often in the night and when she did, she checked them all again. At one time she stooped to check beneath her bed, but was now too brittle and knew one push from one grotesque little hand and she'd topple over and damage something. The way it had happened to her daughter that day at the well.

Stanley could hear Nana at night, the soles of her naked feet like worn slippers shuffling from corner to corner. When he brought this up at supper, she snorted at him.

'I'll want to know if they're in my room, Stanley.' She sat at the table between her granddaughters, no higher than either of them. 'Any fool would want to know that.'

'Ma,' Marigold warned.

Nana turned and brought her face close to Bobbie, who began blinking rapidly. 'They get thirsty, same as anyone, stumbling all over the place at night trying to find their way to the well. They'll come into your room, then not find their way out again.'

'Drop it, Ma,' Marigold said.

Nana scowled at her daughter. 'I let you play too long in the woods. Look what happened to your leg.'

'You're going too far with this,' Stanley said, stretching an arm out for the potatoes that sat just beyond his reach, but no one moved.

'You!' Nana sneered and he withdrew his arm. She pushed her plate away and looked defiantly at her daughter. 'Money will never grow on *his* trees. Mister big shot.'

Marigold sighed. 'Ma.'

But it was just a sound. A sound like something they heard over and over again in the hemlocks at night. Or on the other side of a bedroom wall.

It brings no luck to repeat it, thought Stanley, who often awoke at night and in the summer heat began to turn to Marigold, but stopped, hearing the patter of Nana's feet across her floor. And he would wonder, who was Marigold before the children? Before the accident and her bad leg? Before the two crutches that she separated from so easily, only to find herself stranded and calling out to him for help? Throughout the day he fetched a crutch, he figured, it must be a dozen times.

She'd had the same clear skin, brown eyes, her hair straight and fine. There was nothing special about her, but the first time he had seen her she looked like a young girl, the way some girls looked in those days, not happy, not sad, just waiting to grow up. Now he can't remember that, and at night she sleeps on her good side, the scarred reduced hip a barrier between them.

* * *

Stanley sleeps late. The screens mute the chatter of his daughters, of the metallic clink of utensils in the kitchen cottage below, of several blue jays and a single wood thrush.

Marigold comes in through the sunlight caught in the doorway and hands him his coffee. It's only half a cup, the rest having sloshed out as she came up the steps to the sleeping cottage.

She straightens out his clothes, throws the dirty ones into the yard, hangs the rest on nails driven into the raw unpainted walls.

'Gypsy moths are back,' she says, removing an ashtray from her dresser top. He begins to stir, then is forced to shut his eyes as she blows away the grey ash scattered among her lipstick, nail file and comb.

'Sit back, Stan. Nana's already talking about your can of poison. Her breathing's been irregular all morning. You can't do a thing about those gypsy moths when they come. Nature will have its way.'

She pivots in the centre of the room without her crutch to face him. 'Stanley, she'll put me out of my mind if you start in with that spraying.'

When he won't look at her, she snatches the empty cup and saucer from his hands.

But he knows she likes those creatures no more than he does. Only caterpillars now, black and ugly, they'll cover everything: roofs, clothesline, car, even the rickety wharf fingering its way out over the lake. Denude the trees entirely.

'Another modern gadget,' Nana says scornfully.

Three feet high, steel painted green, an attached hose with power nozzle, Stanley's tank fills with insecticide. He stands over it, legs spread, and pumps up the pressure. He grips the metal handle with one hand, with his other points the nozzle over the cottages and showers the surrounding vegetation with a sticky, unpleasant-smelling tonic. He enjoys the strength of the slender hose, the tremendous height that he is able to make the poison reach.

Nana takes the laundry off the line and Marigold closes the warped shutters on the outside of the sleeping cottage. But they can't do anything about the lower cottage, the shutters there are too heavy for Marigold and Nana to manoeuvre. They could be crushed bringing them down.

Nana empties the kettle of spring water into the sink, afraid it will become contaminated. She sits on the floor with her daughter and granddaughters, away from the windows.

'Damn you, Stanley,' Marigold whispers.

'He's getting back at you,' Nana says.

Bobbie looks up. 'What's Nana mean?'

Marigold dismisses her with a quick shake of her head. She lights a cigarette but it tastes odd. She puts it out, furious.

Outside, the substance drips from the leaves of a young sassafras tree.

'Finished!' Stanley shouts.

'Can we go out now?' Lydia asks.

Stanley has stood the empty tank beside the kitchen door and is flushing it out with the garden hose. The overflowing water runs down the path to the lake.

'Don't play around that water,' Marigold warns her daughters.

'Christ, Marigold, this is perfectly safe. Friggin' female hysteria.' Stanley leaves the water running inside the tank while he has a few drinks on the front porch. He skips lunch. Nearing supper, he refills the tank.

Marigold slices the summer squash, generously covering it with water and salt in a saucepan. Through the kitchen window above the sink she watches him.

Nana is already sitting down, hungry. 'Do you want a place set for him?' she asks.

'Guess not,' Marigold answers. 'I don't know where he's got himself to.'

'Put this back in the cupboard,' Nana says, handing his plate to

Bobbie. 'Right after we eat, one of you girls got to fetch the spring water. We can't forget that.'

There's no sign of Stanley during supper. While they do the dishes, Nana disappears. Marigold lights a cigarette, leaning on a stool for support. She studies the lake, its surface in the dusk like a smooth stone.

She hears Nana's footsteps hurrying back up to the cottage. 'He's going to spray the well,' Nana says, standing outside the kitchen and sputtering through the screens. 'He told me so. He's awful intoxicated, Marigold.'

Marigold is out the door and making her way along the footpath still damp from the spray, when she hears the door open behind her.

'Mom?'

Bobbie is standing in the path.

'Can I come?'

'Certainly not. You don't have anything on your feet.'

'Mom,' Bobbie begs. She is waiting there, in shorts and torn shirt, too thin; her knees, elbows and wrists too prominent; her eyes, in this light, too dark.

'Go back inside,' Marigold says gently. 'Go on. The mosquitoes will eat you alive.' She waits on the narrow path, her back to the cottage, until she hears the kitchen door open and click shut behind her, then makes her way with care over the dirt ground now blackened by shadow. The light reflected up from the lake is growing weak.

Marigold spots her husband on the fieldstone steps that lead over the hill to the well. She thinks of her father, decades ago, putting in these steps, hacking at the ground with an axe and when he was finished, getting down on his knees to sneak the tubers of day lilies into the earth. Although no one tends the lilies now, they thrive, and it is here, surrounded by orange and yellow flowers whose single day of bloom is now ending, that Stanley is struggling with the tank, unaware that the power nozzle is caught several feet below him on a railing support.

As she reaches the base of the steps he collapses, his legs suddenly unable to support him, the tank too heavy.

'Stanley.'

His expression, he knows, is relief. He waits on his knees for her to come up, then lays a hand on her apron, over her bad leg.

'Dear,' he says, softly. 'You drive me up the friggin' wall.'

'Get up, Stanley. You're upsetting Nana, and you look ridiculous.' It's not, after such a long day, what he was expecting her to say. Not what he was hoping for. 'Marigold. Think about it.' 'Surely you don't really expect us to move?'

'Of course not, dear,' he says automatically, then imagines freeing the power nozzle and spraying her tiny feet, one not quite flat on the steps below him. Instead, he reaches down, lifts the tank, and heads up over the hill towards the well.

SUNKEN ISLAND

THE SUN FELL in a yellow slant through the hemlocks and blazed my eager back as though this were its first day on earth. Within minutes, it would travel up the oilcloth and puddle over my poached eggs, creamed corn and sweet tea – flavours that would stay on my tongue all morning.

'Today's the day, you two,' my grandmother said to us, her voice raspy, feeble, because it was so early. 'To Sunken Island and back again.' She hobbled towards us from the cookstove, the sound of her slippered feet like rain pattering in a straight track across the floor.

An hour later my grandmother sat at the stern of the rowboat in grey skirt and pale blue jersey, her crutch sticking out behind her. The boy who did the yard work rowed.

I swam in the water beside them.

I thought of my sister Harriet slipping from the breakfast table and vanishing, mute to my grandmother's threats called out across the hillside. Her place was here, alongside me, but instead she lay hiding beneath a cot in one of the empty cottages, her long unbrushed hair now sticky with cobwebs.

The boy pulled the oars onto his lap and sat without moving as the bow of the boat nudged Sunken Island. My grandmother exhaled cigarette smoke and said, 'Well, Lucy, you've made it this far.'

Sunken Island was this: a pile of algal-green rocks, a dead island licked again and again by clear lake water. The smell that arose from it was as fishy and sour as the dishrag that hung from a single nail beneath our kitchen sink. I circled it widely, afraid to touch it with my bare skin, then began swimming back towards the green smudge that was shore. Silken bubbles formed, burst and uncurled against my skin.

The rowboat followed closely. When I looked up and saw my grandmother watching me I was not surprised. Smoke twisted out her nose as she tossed her cigarette onto the water and I imagined its sogginess, the sound it made as it sizzled on the surface of the lake somewhere near me. Suddenly, I was aware of my grandmother's deep, unmistakable unhappiness; of the fact that there was a part of her that did not, after all, want me to succeed at this test.

The taste of my breakfast grew stronger in my mouth. I stalled, treading the water gently, and felt the coolness of the lower reaches of the lake surrounding my feet.

My grandmother spoke to the boy, then bent towards me over the stern of the boat, extending her crutch for my hands to take.

'Tell me again, how it happened,' Harriet said.

It was the first week of summer. Harriet and I were sitting on a bed in the sleeping cottage, watching our mother dress for a doctor's appointment. She had just come out of the lake.

'It was an accident,' my mother said. 'You know that, Harriet.'

My mother was putting on her bra, the way she always did, with her back to us. She fastened it at the front and then twisted it around, poking her arms through the straps and lifting the cups into place. When she turned back to us she said, 'She slipped on the ice. She didn't heal well. It was before you were born. End of story.'

Then she smiled, and sat down between us, reaching out to tuck my bangs behind my ears. 'Wash your hair at swimming time,' she said to me, then looked at Harriet. 'Both of you.'

'It's a pretty dress,' I told her, and we all looked down at it: sleeveless, with brown and orange flowers against which my mother's glossy, tanned body seemed camouflaged. She smelled fresh, of shampoo, lotion, powder and her own still-hot skin. But it was impossible for me to decipher her odour, to pick out the parts.

The sleeping cottage was a maze of connecting rooms, dim and safe, even at midday. It was here each night that Harriet and I, washed and ready for bed, waited under plaid flannel blankets for our grandmother to come up to us.

We would hear the sound of the kitchen door squeaking as it opened then slapped shut again, and of my grandmother, stepping out into the night. I would sit up and press my face to the screen and watch her where she paused below, checking her apron pockets for cigarettes. She limped the short distance towards the stairs that led up to us, then took the hand rail and climbed slowly, one step at a time, carrying her crutch.

She entered the room with an outstretched hand, lurching towards one of our cots. When she sat at my side I could smell the wood and rubber of her crutch, and the smoky sweetness of her pockets.

Each night she told us the same stories she had heard as a child, mostly about the lake fairy, a small winged creature once seen by her own mother.

'Have you seen her too?' we would ask.

'No, dear, never. She's patient business.'

Naturally, I searched for the lake fairy during the day, wading along the lake's edge where mysteriously there was no beach, where the slender trees seemed to sprout from the water itself. And I waited for her at night, while the wind scratched at the hemlocks above and Harriet breathed rhythmically in her sleep. I hoped she might climb the outside of the cottage and cling to the mesh of the screen windows with her tiny hands; that, if asleep, I might somehow know to awake and see her there, watching us.

The stories ended when my grandmother's cigarette ash had grown long and was bending, dry and grey, above her cupped hand, and we would drift off hearing the lake lap the shore, the hot click of insects in the trees.

Harriet and I knew not to expect visitors. Outsiders were rarely welcomed by my grandmother and were allowed access to our lives only when necessary, and always with disapproval. She complained to us of the boy who came to stack the wood and rake the yard: *Why doesn't he wash his hair?* she asked us, as though such a simple act would bring him great rewards. And the woman to whom we brought the laundry: *I wish she'd purchase herself some decent clothing, get rid of those rags. Pity she can't sew.*

It was a surprise then when a charcoal-coloured Mercedes arrived one afternoon, travelling so quietly we could hear only the crunch of its tires over the stone drive.

'Damnation,' my grandmother whispered. 'Here comes Carmela.'

'Who's Carmela?' we asked.

Coughing, my grandmother smashed out her cigarette and pushed her crossword puzzle away.

'Who's Carmela?'

'Lucy, don't shout. She's nobody. I used to play with her. Hand me my crutch, dear. I better get out and meet her or she'll be coming in.'

My grandmother moved as fast as she could, her right shoulder hooked over the top of one crutch and her longer leg hustling. I watched her go over the dirt yard that was worn down as smooth as ice, the ball of her foot on her shorter leg coasting easily across it. Sunlight came down through the tall trees, frayed and peaceful, grazing her shoulders, brown skirt, her navy-blue sneakers.

Carmela stepped from her car and moved quickly when she saw that my grandmother was already outside.

They kissed, and Carmela handed her a small basket.

'I wish you wouldn't do this,' my grandmother said gratefully.

Carmela was making soft clucking sounds, running her flattened palms over her skirt and blouse in a manner more ladylike than anything I'd ever seen from my grandmother.

'Keep some for yourself,' my grandmother offered. 'This is too much.'

'I've got plenty. Believe me. Plenty.'

'You're too generous. You shouldn't bring them every year.'

Carmela was looking around. Finally she spotted us sitting on the porch floor behind the screens.

'Marigold, are those two big girls your granddaughters?'

My grandmother nodded.

'That big already? Isn't that lovely.'

'Yes. They're with me for a spell.'

Carmela was smiling.

'Bobbie is in for an operation,' my grandmother said at last.

'About time, too, from what I've been hearing, Marigold.'

'I never see the advantage,' my grandmother said, in a voice unsteady but familiar to me, 'to turning everything into an emergency.'

Carmela directed towards us a brief, sympathetic look. 'My niece Lizzie? You remember her, Marigold. I think it would be a lovely idea if she came out here for a while. Give you a hand. Her mother tells me she's bored silly this summer.'

'Please. Don't bother with anything like that.'

'Now, Marigold, I know you. It's clear you need some help around here.'

'I don't need any such thing.' But for a moment my grandmother would not meet this woman's eyes. It was when she smiled that I saw how angry she was.

Carmela left, and we followed my grandmother into the kitchen, curious to discover what was in the basket. She held it out to us, then drew it back when we tried to reach inside. 'Every summer that damn woman brings me red raspberries. Maggoty with seeds. Ruin your teeth.'

'How old's this Lizzie person?' Harriet asked.

'Set the table, girls.'

Harriet grabbed the mismatched plates and glasses from the cupboard and handed them over to me without looking my way. I wanted to catch her eye but she was moving quickly, running around the table slapping down the knives, forks and spoons.

'Put some order to it, Harriet,' my grandmother said.

'How old is this Lizzie?' Harriet asked again, backing away from the table.

My grandmother turned towards the window that looked out across the lake. 'Why couldn't that woman have left us alone?'

I set the plates down carefully, rearranging the cutlery, folding the paper napkins into perfect sails and tucking them safely beneath the plates. We each had a favourite plate, even my grandmother. Harriet's was one-of-a-kind, with peach-coloured roses and faded vines, scalloped edges and minute, delicate cracks. Mine was not one-of-a-kind. It had a vibrant red unidentified flower in the centre and was one of several that my grandmother also claimed as her favourite.

My mother's was blue, light blue and so old nothing of the original pattern could be seen. We were keeping it at the bottom of the stack until she returned.

It was hot, the day following Carmela's visit. Usually we were safe from the heat under the tall hemlocks, beside the lake. But the sun came down and found us, especially my grandmother. She easily grew weak and pink-faced on these days.

Then, mid-morning, Carmela returned with her niece, who was driving the Mercedes. She parked it far up on the dirt drive on a patch of lime-green moss my grandmother preferred us not to walk across.

'True to my word, Marigold,' Carmela said, sailing over to us. 'I've brought you some help. Lizzie loves to work.'

'I just love children,' Lizzie said.

We stared openly at Lizzie. She had blond hair that looked as though someone had spent the morning brushing it, stroke after stroke after stroke. She was wearing pressed white shorts with a flowered turned-up hem, and a matching white blouse with a flowered collar and flowered turned-up sleeves. She was glamorous.

My grandmother had both crutches with her. She was sagging between them. Her hair had fallen out on her neck and her face was no longer pink, but more the colour of vanilla ice-cream, like her bad leg.

'I honestly do not need —'

'Don't be a goose, Marigold.'

'Carmela, listen to me.'

'People love to help you.'

My grandmother shifted, rearranging her weight over her crutches. 'This heat is merciless.'

'It's the humidity,' Lizzie said.

'But notice, Lizzie, how lovely and cool it is down here,' Carmela said. 'It's hot as the blazes in town, Marigold. You're lucky to still have this place.'

My grandmother transferred one of her crutches to her other side in order to free an arm, and began patting her apron pockets. 'Damn,' she whispered.

'What's that?' Carmela asked.

'My cigarettes. I left them inside. Damn, and damn again.'

There was a brief silence. 'Good heavens, Lizzie,' Carmela said. 'What are you standing there for? Go fetch Marigold's cigarettes.'

'Well, where are they?'

My grandmother hesitated. She studied Lizzie from head to toe. 'On the card table, at the end of the porch,' she said at last.

Lizzie trotted inside. Carmela looked relieved. 'Believe me, I'll have a word with her about what's expected.'

'For cripes sake, don't bother,' my grandmother said, no longer looking at Carmela. She took the cigarette pack from Lizzie. Her mouth tightened around the cigarette as she lit it.

'So it's settled,' Carmela said. 'I'll bring Lizzie back with her things tomorrow.'

My grandmother nodded. She exhaled, scanning the far shore of the lake.

Because of the heat we were allowed to go skinny-dipping that night, just before bed.

Harriet and I carried down a bar of soap and towels. Behind us, our grandmother followed, her crutches swishing against the leathery-leafed mountain laurel. When we went into the water we went carefully, not speaking, using memory to feel our way over the rocky bottom of the black water.

The lake sucked away the heat from my body and I imagined it might feel like this standing on another world, where the air might be like water, where everything might touch you in a changed, but pleasant way.

I turned and searched the shore for my grandmother. The off-and-on red glow of her cigarette was the only indication that she stood there at the water's edge, disguised by vegetation and by night. Yet somehow her presence was as clear as day to me, as though her spirit were the strongest thing about her.

I knew that she would swim later, after we were asleep. She cherished her time in the water, floating on her back, her grey hair loose around her while she gazed at the sky. She was so light, she seemed almost to rest on the surface of the water without penetrating it.

But as I lay in bed that night I thought of her making her way back down to the lake, her arms hooked over the tops of her crutches, her slender arms working to carry her. I thought how strong those arms must be to have supported her for so long, yet the sight of that bend at her elbows always stirred in me a combination of feelings I was unable to name.

I prayed she would not slip in the dark before reaching the lake.

Lizzie was sixteen years old and there was little about her my grand-mother could fault. Her clothes were not rags and she washed her hair every night in the sink. Although my grandmother repeatedly remarked how ridiculous she was not to bathe in the lake like the rest of us, in the long run I believe she was relieved to have her. The only complaint I ever heard her make about Lizzie was that she was boy-crazy.

'Like a dog in heat,' my grandmother said. 'Imagine a girl her age going around with a twenty-six-year-old man. It takes no stretch of the imagination to wonder why they packed her off to me.'

But Harriet and I fell immediately in love with her. We marvelled as she put away her clothes.

'Shoot, this is nothing,' Lizzie told us. 'You oughta see what's left at home. If that house burns down on me? I'll kill someone.'

At night Lizzie flew up the steps to the sleeping cottage, telling us our grandmother was too tuckered out from the day we had given her to come up herself. I found this difficult to accept, for these were the same days we had always given her. And now she had Lizzie to help with the groceries, the laundry, the constant sweeping and mopping.

Perhaps if I had complained, my grandmother's response would have allowed me to see how troubled she was that summer. Perhaps I would have even perceived – however distantly – that this was to be my last summer at the lake, that I would never hear anyone speak of the lake fairy again, never hear my grandmother's cool whispered words describing her.

'Show us your boobs,' Harriet said to Lizzie the second night.

'Mind your beeswax,' Lizzie returned lazily.

'I just want to see what they look like.'

'You'll get your own some day.'

'I want to see what they look like now.'

'Show us,' I begged.

'Well, all right. Turn that light off.' She sounded as though she just wanted to get the thing over with. She lifted her blouse and there was her bra, edged with pretty pink lace.

'No!' Harriet said. 'Your boobs.'

Lizzie smirked and reached behind to unfasten her bra just as Harriet sprung into the air and yanked the light back on. For a moment I saw swing free two white mounds with dark centres the size of quarters.

'Cheater,' Lizzie said in a different voice, both resentful and tolerant. She took her time putting herself back together, then whispered, 'Go to sleep.'

Harriet and I lay without speaking in the dark. I had often seen my grandmother naked, stripping out of her wet suit after swimming. But she did not have anything like those on her chest. Her body was wrapped in thin folds that were like waves. Except for her scar, which ran deeply inwards at the top of her bad leg.

Almost every night thereafter Lizzie crossed the room and in the dimming light exposed herself to us. Eventually she did not need to be coerced but came to us, waiting until all that any one could hear was the occasional buckle of a slack screen or chirp of a lone cricket in the closet, and lifted her blouse. She turned first slightly towards Harriet, then shifted back towards me, so that we were allowed the privilege of viewing her from all angles. In that just-past-dusk light, the kitchen lights coming up from the cottage below yellow and starchy, Lizzie's breasts might have been marble rather than flesh, but though Harriet asked, we were never given permission to touch them.

As she released her blouse her hands floated to her hips like discarded gloves. When I realized she was removing her bra in preparation for these visits, a peculiar excitement swept through me, as if my role was, in some way, one of complicity.

But Lizzie had a manner of exposing her body and describing details of what she and her boyfriend had done – beneath trees and bushes in broad daylight – that stilled me with a secret terror. Anxiously, I began to imagine the way my own body would change, the events that could, some day, happen to me.

Lizzie knew other things too.

One night she told us our grandmother had attended university for a year.

'Why?' I asked.

'To be a mathematician. If you can believe that.'

'A what?' I asked.

'Adding, subtracting, long division, short division. Aunt Carmela says she was a real hotshot.'

'Is she still?'

'Gawd no, Lucy. Does she look like one? Too bad she went and fell down on that old ice. I bet she hates winter.'

'Why would she hate winter?'

'You don't understand anything, Lucy,' Harriet said.

'Aunt Carmela says she couldn't have her cake and eat it too. Take a look around you. That's why no one in your family has a real life.'

'I have a real life,' I insisted.

But Lizzie only stared at us, her expression indulgent, her fingers restless with the hem of her blouse.

One day towards the end of summer Lizzie packed up and left, back to her boyfriend and her wardrobe. That evening my grandmother, Harriet and I carried birthday candles and paper baking cups down to the shore. We melted the ends of the candles and stuck them upright inside the cups, then set them in the water. My grandmother used her crutch to gently push them off, out beyond the danger of the small breaking waves.

We waited and watched, and after a while the water was lit by the yellow lights of a dozen candles heading across the lake in baking cups. Eventually most went out, either burned down or capsized, but several continued on, blinking precariously.

My grandmother whispered, 'Almost all the way to Sunken Island, girls.'

The following day I tried to swim to Sunken Island and back again. This time I did not stall halfway to shore, dropping my legs under me in the deep water and reaching out for my grandmother's crutch. Instead I swam with an unfamiliar determination that in itself was so frightening I almost stopped. But there had been something distancing me from my grandmother all summer – perhaps Lizzie's demonstrations at bedtime while my grandmother remained below, tired and worried – that allowed me now to ignore her as she sat smoking in the rowboat. I kept my eyes on the rim of the lake where the leafy shore came down to meet the rocks, staring so hard that after a while I saw a tiny figure drifting among the trees.

I panicked, and almost stopped. Then it came to me that here, at last, was the lake fairy, just as my grandmother had described her: pretty and strong, wearing a white dress, hovering over the tops of the trees. I heard my grandmother's crutch bang loudly on the metal side of the boat, but I continued on, watching instead the lake fairy until she disappeared among the vegetation.

Finally, my feet touched the floor of the lake. In the cold shade covering the bare earth I looked up towards the cottages and saw that my mother had returned.

The rowboat jabbed the shore behind me and my grandmother said, 'Lucy, hurry now and get a towel. You'll catch your death.'

I had not seen my mother for over a month. When I went to meet her I almost didn't recognize her. I looked at her breasts, at the shape they made through her pink jersey. It was impossible to tell which one they had taken.

'I just swam to Sunken Island and back again,' I told her as she wrapped a towel around me.

'Oh,' she said. 'I was never able to do that.'

MOVIE CHILDREN

IN THE EARLY MORNING we leave Goose Bay. Estelle immediately begins insisting that our pilot, Ray, fly us inland over a particular river canyon. She has been told that there, on steep grey-green walls, we might see falcons crouched over eggs in nests that are nothing more than a few sticks in rock-smooth cupboards.

It has been over a year since my wife and I became devoted to bird-watching, but only weeks since I finally lost the last of my enthusiasm. She keeps up with the adventure and I play my part, sitting in the back of the helicopter, my mind on other things.

Though sometimes, Estelle daydreams too. While I pretend to look through my binoculars, I watch her peer down between her legs through the clear bubble of the helicopter and I know that she is enchanted with her own fear, three thousand feet up in the sky. I know that for her there is nothing else but the shake and hum of the helicopter and all of the round, wide world that she can see from it.

I'm rocking around in the brittle early morning light, feeling high and empty and isolated, when Estelle's voice addresses me through my headphones.

'See anything?' she asks. I shake my head and catch her glance at Ray, whose bleached hair hangs down over his tanned forehead.

It is then that Ray and I see them: minute objects far down below us, crawling sluggishly on the flattest section of sandy earth beside the flattest stretch of blue river.

Ray immediately lets the helicopter fall, as though it is some kind of cocoon spiralling down out of the sky, and I watch these things below us become gradually larger, quicker. They are people, running in circles, waving at us, then stopping to brace themselves against the gust of the helicopter's blades. I notice a boat on its side far from the water and closer, little tents made of people huddled under coats and blankets around a small fire. They do not move, not even to have a look at us.

A tall man in a red hunting jacket approaches the helicopter, ducking in under the revolving blades, and starts yelling. 'Ray, how's it goin'?

Motor's seized. Frozen up solid ...' he takes a breath '... since yesterday.'

Ray shakes his head in sympathy. 'Pain in the arse,' he says. 'Radio?'

The man shrugs. 'Radio's broke.'

Ray chuckles.

Estelle grins – she's one of the boys.

'Locate Nita, willya?' the man yells. 'Get her to send someone in with a boat. Don't know if this crowd's gonna make it. Bunch of Swedes. Flies are wicked.'

Ray nods and looks out at the stooped figures. A black screen of insects blurs them. Just then a hood lifts and we see a strange, gutted face, as though it has lost all sense of past and future and knows only the misery of the present. It stares, despising us for sitting in this helicopter, capable at any moment of springing back up into the sky.

Ray turns back to his friend. 'Fly dope?' he asks.

'I'll take anything you wanna give me.'

'No sweat.' Ray slaps his breast pockets and Estelle flies into action, searching all our bags and coming up with two bottles of Muskol.

'Here. I insist you have ours, too,' she says, leaning over Ray, her face passionately earnest and sympathetic.

She glances back at me then, as though she has never forgotten I am there, and gives me a fertile, solitary smile.

Just before the man turns away he remembers something and grins. 'Guess you better inform the wife. Give 'er a shout for me, willya?'

Ray chuckles, Estelle chuckles, and then she yells to Ray, 'So on to that canyon!'

'It's not a choice I'd be makin',' he yells back, not looking at her.

Ray is against flying over this river canyon because there are no floats on the helicopter. If we go down there will be nowhere to land but on the deep still water that fills all these canyons like a sky. All the way down, thousands of feet, the granite walls drop as straight as skyscrapers.

But Estelle is adamant. She is riding high on the fantasy of having just saved a bunch of Swedes with two bottles of insect repellent.

'Hey. Come on. I'm always lucky!' Estelle yells.

We strap back on our headphones and the helicopter lifts, hovers, twirls gracefully. It spins out sideways over the shallow river and rushes the water before it in tiny, powerful crests.

When Ray speaks into the mike he concentrates on the space ahead of him as though he is alone; it is only through some instinct that I know when he is talking to me, and when to Estelle.

'If she goes down,' he says now to Estelle, his voice grave and faraway in my own ears, 'I'll bring her close to the wall. Before we touch water I'll tilt her so she sets down on my side. Then you open your door there and haul out.'

Inside I feel as though I am already racing down, for I know what Estelle's thoughts are churning out now: adventure, rescue, a happy ending.

'You listening?' he asks her.

He doesn't sound friendly, but Estelle doesn't notice.

When we do set down, onto a circle of smooth white rubble above the sea, a pickup is waiting. Out of it pops a woman to whom Ray gives a brief smile. She grabs our bags and carries them over to the truck.

Estelle takes her time getting out of the helicopter, which has immediately become covered with the black bodies of flies and mosquitoes, and I can see that she is watching both Ray and this woman. Fluffy white flowers stand like lollipops all around us, and I wonder when Ray has been here last.

Estelle and I never ask Ray about the sleeping and eating arrangements, and Ray never tells us. So we get into the truck with the woman.

'Isn't Ray coming?' Estelle asks her.

'I'll be back for him. He'll be after doing some work on her yet,' she says, indicating the helicopter. Her smile, shameless, spreads across her face.

She starts up the truck while Estelle sits staring out at a sky and bank of mountains that seem short and unmiraculous from here.

'Ray told me you're right fond of the movies,' the woman says. She is very small, rugged and friendly. 'Sure, I'd go foolish here without them.'

Estelle turns to her. 'He told you that?'

'He told us to pick one up for tonight. For us all. After you settle in, I'll take you to get one.'

Then she says her name is Nita, and that she is the hotel manager.

The hotel is undergoing renovations. We are in a long room with new panelling that is so blond and sweet-smelling I expect sap to run from it. Nita shows us the bathroom, which is half finished – partly dark and rotted, partly lustrous and still sticky from caulking compound.

Nita smiles. She is proud of these changes.

An hour later Ray opens the door and sticks his head in. He has just showered and looks tired, but in a good mood. He says he's stopping in across the hall to have a drink with a couple of the boys he's run into. Then he'll see us at supper. He adds that Nita's got a feed of caribou on, special. He doesn't mention the movie.

Estelle flops down across one of the beds and lets her arm dangle over the side. Her fingers just reach a coarse brown carpet obviously not yet included in the renovations, and she starts to scratch over it with her nails, making an unpleasant sound.

Across the hall the noise level picks up. One person is shouting, telling stories and barely giving anyone else a chance to speak.

Finally the phone between the two beds rings. I wait to see if Estelle will reach for it. She gives me a look instead. I pick it up.

It's Nita. She tells me she's all set to get that movie.

I look at Estelle. She shakes her head. 'You go,' she whispers. 'Get anything.'

As I stand the phone rings in the room across the hall and Estelle and I glance at each other. We both assume it's Nita, this time looking for Ray.

But when I leave the hotel a few minutes later Nita is already in her truck waiting. She looks damp and, like Ray, must have just showered. Her wet, strawberry-blond hair is pulled up on top of her head in a confusing, attractive way.

She bumps us along over the potholed road, which consists of yellow hard-packed dirt and is without definition, like a river passing through this community. It washes up to the fronts of buildings, eliminating what might have been yards, and circles the ratty spruce trees that grow in small groups like islands.

We pass a group of Inuit children swarming over a rusted truck. Some are in the back, others are crowded into the cab, while one, a girl, is standing on the roof and another is climbing out a window. A younger boy, too small to get into the truck by himself, holds a gleaming fishing pole over a brown trickle of water that runs through the dirt yard. He is wearing blue rayon shorts that are tight over his soft legs. He bobs the fishing pole up and down with a look on his smudged face that is thoughtful, almost grim.

Nita asks me if we have any children. I tell her, no, we haven't been lucky ... we've been waiting a long time.

Nita smiles broadly and says, 'Sure, you got each other. Be thankful for what you got.'

Then she tells me that she has a two-year-old daughter. When I look surprised she adds that her husband is back in the country, cutting wood. She swings the truck up inches from a pink clapboard building and I stare at it, thinking about what Nita cannot know, about the many, tiny, unpaired genes within me.

After Estelle and I were married two years we began seeing doctors. When the last tests were over we came home, unable to speak to each other. After a while Estelle went out.

When she returned she said, 'If I cannot conceive and bear children, I don't want to know anyone who can.'

The inside of the store is dark. I don't see any videos. With the exception of a few candy bars and bags of chips on a wooden counter, I see nothing that I would expect to find in a store. But I do see the children, silent and aloof as they watch me.

At least two dozen young Inuit are in this room. Some are in front of the counter, some behind it, some on it. One girl is sitting next to the cash register with her legs dangling inside the counter so that her back is to me. Her hair is long, black, lying across her shoulders in small knots. She turns and watches me with less hesitancy than the others. Suddenly she smiles and says 'Hi,' like a bark, and I'm caught off guard.

Then Nita is beside me, telling the woman behind the counter that we want the movies. The woman hands me a box stacked with videos and I carry them over to a scarred wooden table. Most are horror or pornographic in jackets that are worn and faded. I try to think what Estelle would like, as Nita, who has seen all of them several times, makes some recommendations. We decide on a romantic comedy.

I take the video to the counter. The woman asks for three dollars and seems relieved when our transaction goes smoothly. She stares at me, then smiles shyly.

Suddenly I imagine that I stay with this gentle woman and together we raise stout, sturdy children with sleek skin and blessed eyes. We burrow away here happily through snowy winters and insect summers, with the sky low and heavy and safe over us.

On the way back to the hotel we pass the truck again, but the children have moved over to a short bumpy hill where they are holding a beat-up stroller and discussing something. Behind them is an inlet, flat and dark, somehow not reflecting any sunlight. It looks more like scuffed-up linoleum than water. A brown mangy dog is digging in the dirt nearby, and I am reminded of Estelle scraping her fingernails over the hotel carpet.

The children appear to make a decision. They put the smallest among them – the boy with the blue rayon shorts – into the stroller, then run with it down the hill towards the water and push it off. The boy goes bouncing and flopping away over the knobby grass while the brown dog lopes after him, barking. Alarmed, I twist in my seat as we pass but lose sight of the stroller just as it slows and begins to tip. Something pulls inside of me, feelings that are familiar but unwelcome – sadness and fiery longing.

Then I remember the woman in the store, her nutty skin, the smooth slope of her cheeks. I imagine her watching the stroller and laughing, and realize that my own fantasies are not so unlike Estelle's.

When Estelle and I go in for supper Ray is already there with two friends, a small Nigerian and his pilot, an American.

I can tell right away that it was the Nigerian doing all the shouting. He immediately begins speaking to Estelle, explaining he's a botanist employed by the government. He and his pilot spend the day flying from one randomly chosen plot to another, collecting moss and lichen in ziplock bags. During the day it is enormously boring, but now, he says, it seems hilarious. Except for missing his family.

The Nigerian's pilot is smoking and studying Estelle. He tells her that his wife Emily has just had their first baby. Premature. It was a strange looking thing, like something he once found fallen out of a tree. A squirrel fetus, he thinks it was.

The Nigerian pats his pilot on the back. 'He talks too much. It's because he's crazy. What in hell is a squirrel fetus doing on the ground?'

The pilot runs his fingers through his stiff yellow hair and scans the table, not looking at any of us. 'I said I thought it was a squirrel. It was hairless. It had real skin, like human skin. Its eyes didn't open.' He carefully snuffs out a half-finished cigarette and returns it to the pack. He nudges the Nigerian. 'Come on, let's get another bottle.'

The Nigerian turns to Estelle. Does she have any babies?

When she says, no, he sighs, 'Ah,' and cocks his head. 'How long you married?'

She tells him the truth, four years.

'Come on, man,' the pilot says.

'That long? Ah ... you sure no babies?' the Nigerian asks her, grinning like this is the funniest thing in a long time.

Estelle grins too. 'I'm sure,' she says.

For a moment I wonder if maybe this is funny.

'I know that. I know that, just looking at you. What about him?' the Nigerian asks, indicating Ray.

Estelle says she doesn't think so.

'Hey you, Ray! Hey!' the Nigerian shouts. 'You make any babies?'

Ray laughs. He is hunkered over his plate, eating. He looks at the Nigerian and winks. The Nigerian gets such a kick out of this that all of his delicate body shakes with it.

'I'm goin', man,' the Nigerian's pilot says, rising.

'Hey, you wait!' The Nigerian stands. 'Don't drink all my whisky.' He turns back to Estelle. 'He's crazy.'

Ray finishes his meal quickly. Just before leaving he says to me, 'Come on back to the room for a drink, if you've a mind to.'

'I don't know.'

'Come on, boy,' he says, as though this is ridiculous. He doesn't look at Estelle.

Outside it's as bright as noonday. A few dusty birch trees are moving just beyond the windows; through them the light is hitting the room in quick splashes, coming and going all over Estelle's legs.

After a while she asks, 'Did you hear him today, talking about crashing?'

'There's little chance of that.'

'At least I feel safe. In case we do go down.'

I look her over. I want to stop myself, but I go on. 'I can't figure why he gave you that baloney.'

'What do you mean?'

I twist my lips over to one side and finger the skin around one corner of my mouth, a habit Estelle doesn't care for. 'If he brought the copter down onto her side like that the blades would be thrown off when they hit the water. There's a good chance they'd come crashing in and slice apart the person sitting next to the pilot.'

'Are you sure?'

'It's a possibility.'

'Doesn't Ray know that?'

'You'd think.'

Yes, sometimes I am like a child, believing that I can get away with these things. 'Listen,' I say. 'They're all getting together now. You don't mind, do you?'

'It's up to you.'

'It's up to you.'

'Go ahead. I've got that movie to watch with Nita anyway.'

For a couple of hours I sit with the boys in the room across the hall from the one where Estelle and Nita watch the movie. I get a little blotto and spend most of the time staring through our partly opened door at their closed one. I listen to the Nigerian, who is less clear now but still going on and on. Every once in a while Ray gives him shit over something and they all yell and open another beer.

Then the door across the hall opens and Nita comes out. She doesn't look at us, but with her head down, begins to turn and go.

'Where you headin' off to?' Ray shouts at her.

'Office. Paperwork's piled a mile high.' She smiles at us.

A few minutes later Ray stands. He excuses himself and there follow loud, cussing protests. Then it's just the unstable thumping of his footsteps as he goes down the hall.

When Estelle comes out she doesn't look in at us either, but I can see by her face that it will take her a while to shake off the movie. Even light movies affect her.

I sit where I am, on the edge of a blue cooler packed with bags of moss and lichen, and tell myself that it's no longer any of my business. But I don't really believe that. So I go down the hall, too. I pass through the empty dining room where the tables have not yet been cleared from supper.

Down another hallway I see my wife disappear into Nita's office. I get as far as the doorway.

Ray is standing with his back to us, leaning against the outside wall with his hands pressed around a window. He looks unsteady, but tense, preoccupied. The light of night is streaming in around him.

Suddenly Nita moves. Crouched slightly, she could be a boxer caught between Ray's chest and the window. She sees Estelle from beneath his armpit and begins to give her that broad smile, but just then Ray puts his hands on her arms and tosses her once, playfully, against the window. Her face moves out of sight as the glass panes rattle.

Somehow Ray senses Estelle and he turns. It takes him a moment to focus on her, then he scowls, as though he has been insulted.

It's near midnight when I return to our room. The shade has been drawn and Estelle is in bed. I hesitate, then carefully approach and lean over her, trying to see her face.

Outside, a group of children wander by, their voices rushed and businesslike. A girl begins screaming angrily. Then I hear giggles and the slapping sound of their bare feet as they run off.

'Estelle?' I whisper.

She speaks, but I can't make it out. She sounds too small, too far away.

I kneel and drop over her until my cheek rests on her stomach. It has been a long time since I have touched her in this way.

After a while she says, 'I don't feel like flying up any more river canyons.'

I lift my head and look across at the window shade where slices of light are coming in around it as though from another planet. 'Too much for you?' I ask.

'What do you mean?' she asks sharply.

Suddenly I feel shaky, unfixed to the earth, like the little boy bounding down the hill in the beat-up stroller. 'I just wondered if everything … the flying, the people …' Then I know what I mean. 'Maybe we ask for too much?'

We stare at each other. In this light that is neither night nor day her eyes are a strange colour: a stony, fleeting, prized blue.

'Estelle,' I say, impulsively, 'love me forever.'

But for a moment I want to give up, and she sees it.

PILGRIMS

CHARLIE STANDISH AVERY was descended from mighty people. From Myles Standish himself, and from Barbara, the woman Myles married when he couldn't marry Priscilla, although Great-Aunt Rebecca said there was no truth to that romance. When Myles left Plymouth for Foxburrough, she said, you can be damn sure he had better things on his mind than young girls.

Great-Aunt Rebecca worshipped those Pilgrims.

'Pilgrims?' Charlie's mother, Ruth, would say. 'You can trace the balance of my unhappiness to those Pilgrims.'

But during Thanksgiving dinner Ruth could rattle off the *Mayflower* passenger list, including all the women who died, and all the children – the oldest girl, of course, being Priscilla Mullins.

When Myles Standish died he left behind one fowling gun, feather beds, sheets, pillows, two saddles, one beer cask, brass kettle, warming and frying pan, Homer's Iliad, Wilson's Dictionary, Turkish History, Burroughs's Christian Contentment –

'Your mother has an impressive memory,' Great-Aunt Rebecca would interrupt, her glass beads clanking against her dinner plate.

At this, Rebecca's younger sister, Great-Aunt Sarah, who usually wasn't home because, as Rebecca put it, she was addicted to sailing, would reach over and pat Rebecca's wrist, and Rebecca would flick her off.

Charlie's mother had been raised by these two women in one of three poky houses lining Pilgrim Byway. The Byway connected two main roads and ran the length of the Myles Standish Cemetery, where Myles was buried side by side with Barbara. The central portion of the house had originally been a cranberry shed; cramped additions had been added to either side by Rebecca and Sarah's father shortly after they were born. The house was dark, with low ceilings and diamond-shaped leaded windows.

June of the year that Charlie turned thirteen, with school nearly out, his mother suggested he visit his great-aunts in Foxburrough for a while.

'Why?'

'It's Sarah, Charlie. Rebecca says all these years of sailing haven't done anyone any good. She says it might help to have a youngster around the house again. Basically, we *all* have some tough decisions to make. But I think we've learned a lot, don't you? Your father just has a few little things he needs to face. Don't roll your eyes at me. Think of the fun you'll have down at the cottage.'

'Dad can't help it.'

But she shook her head and closed her eyes. 'No,' she said. 'I'm not listening.'

* * *

The cottage was a one-room rickety structure that hung along the parting of the oak woods from the salt meadows that fringed the inside of Foxburrough Bay. At high tide the cold water inched its way up over the marsh grass until it slopped a foot or so below the floorboards, turning the air cool and ocean-rank, especially at night. At low tide another landscape emerged; the water could only be reached via the long boardwalk that fingered out over the marsh, and even then, if it were very low, it was not water that one met but mucky flats with a powerful stench and slippery puckered surface over which black horseshoe crabs dragged one another, locked in intercourse.

Rebecca brought Charlie down to the cottage on his first day. Sarah had been up and gone early and was likely puttering around the yacht club, a take-out beverage in hand as she insinuated herself into discussions with strangers about storm jibs and binnacles.

'Good gracious me, Charlie, look at the growth. I haven't stepped foot here since last summer with you and Donny. Too cold for swimming?'

'Swimming?' Charlie looked out across the salt meadow. He hated swimming here. He hated the razor-sharp eel grass and weird creatures that grazed his body as he did the breaststroke. 'It's dead low,' he said.

Rebecca lurched up the steps to the cottage then paused to catch her breath. She wore a huge, tight-fitting floral dress, the zipper undulating the length of her front. Charlie watched her glass beads sway in that space below her considerable breasts and realized, with horror, that he was becoming aroused.

'Indeedie it is,' she said at last. 'We'll have to come back another day.' She straightened and began moving down the porch towards the door. Charlie watched the structure tremble against the sky.

'Are you sure it's safe, Aunt Rebecca?'

But she was gone inside. He heard the door opening and then her conversation with the empty interior, but although he worried the building might fall he sat down on the bottom step, hoping to shrink that particular part of himself. If he heard crashing and the splintering of wood he could leap away in time, though he knew this was a cowardly thought, to save himself while leaving his great-aunt with a cottage collapsed over her.

One day 'boner' had been just a nasty, giggly word scrawled on desk tops and bathroom walls; the next it was a word for a thing that was dreadfully, unpredictably irresistible.

One winter afternoon his mother had come home and into the house without removing her boots, walked through the kitchen and into his room where he and his brother, Donny, were playing Clue and asked, 'Where's your father?' She was staring at them over the top of a brown paper bag of groceries; her woollen cap had slipped down and covered her eyebrows and she looked cold.

They didn't know. They hadn't seen him for hours although they had heard him in the kitchen stacking the empties.

'I asked him to shovel the driveway.'

She went upstairs and they heard loud voices, but it wasn't until she came stomping back down and into the kitchen where she deposited the groceries on the floor that they could make out her words.

'I can't live with him. Not another minute. I can't live with him. I can't live with him. I can't live with him.'

'Why are you going into the Conservatory, stupid?' Charlie asked Donny. 'I was just there and you *showed* me the card.'

'So what.'

'Well, obviously the murder didn't happen there. Duh.'

'Duh.'

Their mother appeared in the doorway.

Donny leaned back and kicked his legs across the board, scattering the dice, secret envelope, tiny rope, revolver, wrench and candlestick.

Charlie reached over and punched Donny.

'Hey,' his mother warned, sitting on the bed.

Donny began to cry.

'I didn't hit you hard.'

'That's not it,' Donny sobbed, rolling onto his back on the bare floor. Charlie felt his mother holding back; he could feel how she didn't want to love Donny right now. He hated his brother. 'Everyone out of my room!' he said.

'Don't!' Donny cried. 'Don't, Mommy.'

Charlie watched his mother's face soften from wiry anger to exasperation. 'Don't *what?*' she said.

'Don't leave.'

'What are you talking about?'

But they all knew. Charlie wanted to hurt Donny even more now. But he also wanted to hurt his mother. And of course his father. 'Get out of my room!' he shouted and his mother turned and scowled at him. She was thinking, what day is it? How much allowance is left?

'You just lost your allowance,' she said.

'It's gone!' he told her, laughing. 'You already took it away!' And that's when the boner started, when he laughed at her. He felt angry, but powerful, and then guilty. His mother looked away, giving up on him without any allowance to take.

'Don't leave Daddy,' Donny wailed.

'Okay, okay. Come here, baby.' She slipped down onto the floor and Donny crawled across to her. She held him. 'Is that what you think? That I'll leave Daddy?'

Donny nodded. It was so true he couldn't speak it without gagging.

Charlie's mother felt bad now. She rocked Donny in her arms and whispered, 'I promise, baby, I promise. We won't leave him.'

Donny's body bucked slightly. '*I* would stay with Daddy!'

Her eyebrows lifted and the corners of her mouth turned down. She looked up at Charlie sitting on the bed with his pillow clamped over his lap and made a look of pretend despair. 'That would have a lot to recommend it.'

'It's your fault,' Charlie told her.

'My fault? How can you say that?'

'You know he can't shovel the driveway now. It's too late. You should have asked him in the morning. He even wanted to do it in the morning.'

'Why didn't he?'

'You should have reminded him. He can't help it, Mom.'

'So it's my fault?'

'Yes.'

Donny separated from his mother and looked up at her, earnest and hopeful. 'Just don't let him buy any more beer, Mommy.'

She patted Donny. 'Okay, baby.'

Although it was years since she'd slept a single night in the cottage, Rebecca had once spent whole summers here with Sarah, the two of them carrying down little Ruth and boxes of household goods, returning to town only to feed the chickens and shop for food at King's Corner. There was a sweetness to those days, a dewy giddy beauty, and entire weeks when Rebecca and Sarah shared it.

Ruth had been petite, a picky eater. She bit her lip and ground her jaw; they could see her mandibles flex beneath her skin and hear her little teeth grinding at night. Sarah would lie awake, listening. Rebecca would lie awake, irritated with Sarah.

In the evenings they drank Drambuie. Sarah often became ridiculously over-loving with Ruth, and sometimes weepy, but even then, putting the two of them to bed and standing on the porch to follow the last clean-laundry white of sails that clung to the horizon – even then, Rebecca wondered whether she and her family were not just better, but happier, than other people.

Yet it was during those days, when she might have been happiest of all, that a longing to have known her ancestor the soldier Myles Standish first arose. Captain Myles Standish, who migrated from Plymouth Plantation to Foxburrough in 1631 with a single cow.

Rebecca wishes she could have seen the Foxburrough landscape then. To walk across with Myles, Jonathan and Thomas from Plymouth. To see the shad-bush speckle the woods with pink blossoms in spring, the marsh marigolds bloom in carpets along the edge of brooks. The goldenrod, which none of them have seen before, and the Michaelmas daisies. The salt meadows are glossy in the sunshine. At low tide they wander the shore digging up clams and gathering lobsters. She and

Myles sow wheat, peas, beans, and Indian corn. In the fall, the pale orange pumpkins planted among the corn hills are so abundant they carry them, one by one, to store beneath the houses.

Rebecca had forgotten Charlie. It wasn't until she was back outside and the roar of insects, leaves, and water charged her that she wondered, where the blazes is he?

And what in the world would she do with a thirteen-year-old boy for a month? He was too big. Although she had offered to take either of Ruth's sons, she would have preferred Donny.

But there he was, coming out from beneath the weedy sassafras, flushed and overdressed. She was ashamed of herself, but felt an instinctive repugnance at the sight of him, wiping his hands on his trousers. Had Myles looked *anything* like him? It was possible that Myles once ventured along these very paths, bent his head over this same earth, but Rebecca would want Myles to have possessed a greater sense of belonging than Charlie appeared to now, rail-thin and never felt a knife at his throat in his life.

Weak, like his father.

Even today, Rebecca could not bear the thought of Charlie's father's hands on Charlie's mother. Rebecca pictured her own virginity lodged inside her body like a cannon ball: hard and safe, private. Losing it would be like mutating, like succumbing to murder. Like what happened to poor Myles that cold week in Weymouth.

'I thought Ruth looked tired this morning, when she dropped you off,' she said to Charlie now.

'Who? Mom?'

'Yes! Your mother.'

'Nah. She always looks like that.'

'Shame on you.'

'For what?'

'Ruth is capable of looking better.'

Charlie felt surprise, and then guilt.

'Your mother is tired because of your father.'

Charlie heard something and glanced up. The branches of trees met overhead, tossing as though in slow motion.

'Your father is an alcoholic,' Aunt Rebecca said.

'He can't help it.'

'Hello? What if I murdered someone and then said, I can't help it? Would that be my excuse? It's no excuse.'

'Yes, it is.'

'No, you don't know anything. And you're stubborn to boot.'

She paused, eying Charlie, though she knew he was restless to move on, and considered Sarah's mistake. Despite the memory of those summer days, with Ruth dazzling them as she toddled up these porch steps, or studied a leaf or kissed their cheeks, Rebecca remained convinced that having a child – even Sarah's child – was not worth it. Women who give up their virginity, she reflected, you can see right through them.

It was unfortunate that Rebecca was obliged to admit that with his bare hands Myles had committed murder.

Yes, he hesitated. For days. Rebecca admires him for that.

But what could he do? The Plymouth colonists had made him their commander. It mortified Rebecca, to think of those men at Weymouth: undisciplined pioneers roaming the New England woods, half-naked, filthy, starved. First they sell their clothing to the Neponsets, now they're robbing them or, worse, fetching their wood and water in exchange for a capful of corn.

What had happened to Myles that year to make him feel the way he did? Not reckless, but careless. And here, a new world. Yet he felt nothing. He felt that nothing was happening. It was all dull, these dark netted woods of oak, pine, and juniper with their vast flocks of guinea fowl moving in for the winter.

This mood stayed with him at Weymouth. On their arrival his men were aghast to find the white men scattered over the countryside, the Indians gallivanting in and out of their dwellings. But Myles stood apart. Down to the sea margins small pines formed a strange kind of grove: the land was sandy with little undergrowth and the canopy low. They waited several days, the Neponsets lurking and threatening, Myles apathetic and lonely, his men anxious. One evening four Indians circled round him, sharpening their knives, and still he was unmoved. Could he not, at least, take an interest in murder? In his own death pocketed away behind every tree trunk, wigwam, shadow of Indian skittering barefoot across the sand?

Myles bore the head of one of the several Indians he killed back with him to Plymouth. The girl Priscilla Mullins saw it, accidentally.

'What grade, Charlie,' Great-Aunt Sarah asked one mealtime, 'will you be entering this fall?'

'Eight.'

'You must be very smart now.'

'The public school system is a complete waste of the taxpayer's money,' Rebecca said.

'It is?'

'Sarah? Don't you remember? Don't you remember those kooky pilgrim hats and *Mayflower* ships Ruth used to make at Thanksgiving?'

'Maybe.'·

'Eventually we tutored your mother at home, Charlie. Kept her out a few afternoons a week and gave her real history lessons. Stop poking me, Sarah. What a fight I had on my hands with that principal – Mr Forlizzi. She was missing geometry, apparently.'

'She didn't like that,' Sarah said softly.

'Missing *geometry?*'

'No. The arrangement. It embarrassed her.'

'It would sure embarrass me,' Charlie said, without thinking.

His aunts were eating and passing the salt back and forth. But it was – it was crazy!

'He's stubborn,' Rebecca said finally.

'He's not.'

'He is.'

'He's not. He's protecting himself,' Sarah said, her voice distant. Charlie was leaning so far over the table trying to hear her he got succotash on his shirt.

'That's stupid talk, Sarah.' Rebecca rose, moved behind Charlie and reached for his plate, gathering his utensils and plonking them onto it, all the while pressing his shoulder with her side.

Charlie didn't like touching Rebecca, but he didn't want her to know this. Each night when she came to kiss him goodnight, bending over him with her powdery skin, her body squishy and warm, he dutifully thrust his cheek towards her.

But Sarah, standing beside Charlie later that evening at the dining-room window, telling him that when she was a child those woods were cleared so you could see straight down to the cranberry bogs behind the house – those bogs, she added, turned russet in the fall and in the channels the red berries left behind by the raker floated unchecked and were deliciously cold if you bit into one after a frost – Sarah, in her jeans, sneakers and windbreaker, always kept herself at arm's length. If Charlie moved one inch closer, she moved one inch away, not abruptly or immediately but discreetly, as she told him that if you looked closely you could see, beneath the pine needles, the old furrows of tilled soil and the remains of stone walls scattered by neglect and the trunks of powerful oaks.

He couldn't get a whiff of her, let alone a goodnight kiss.

* * *

Days after the Coast Guard departed Foxburrough Harbor, Lionel Hale is still searching for a missing woman whose abandoned sailboat was discovered last Tuesday. The woman, Sarah Standish of No. 3 Pilgrim Byway, is feared dead. According to officials, bloodstains found on the boat indicate Standish may have died of a gunshot wound. Foul play is not suspected.

'That day,' Rebecca told Ruth. 'That day I was down at the cottage, determined to do a little fixing up. I got a splinter under my thumbnail and it gave me a tremendous worry – all out of proportion. I think now it was a premonition. The way I took that splinter so seriously, agonizing over whether a call to Dr DeWolfe was in order? I believe I knew – intuitively – that I would never see Sarah again. Charlie, hand your mother the tissues. You'll be exhausted, Ruth, crying on and on like that. It's a long drive back. And don't bother reading that old paper.'

Sarah Standish was 57. She had never married and had no children.

'That's fine, Ruth. I've read the paper. How I wish Lionel would give up. He's being a hero, that's all, telling the newspapermen she's one of theirs, he won't give up till he finds her body. Oh, that irritates me beyond measure. As though *he* were one of *ours.*'

'Who is he?'

'Lionel? The harbour master. Apparently he has all the facts.'

Only personal items, such as keys, coat and shoes, were found on Standish's boat. The engine was in reverse and still running. The sails were

*down and the centreboard was raised. The boat's dinghy, Baby Ruth, was
still attached.*

'You don't have to repeat it to me, Ruth. Lionel Hale. What a sight
with those long swinging arms, much like an ape.'

'Why don't you like him?' Ruth asked.

'Who said I don't like him?'

'Is he married?'

'Is he married? I believe he is not married.'

'Children?'

'Children? I've no idea. Why do you ask?'

'No reason.'

'Where's Donny?' Charlie asked his mother. 'Why didn't he come?'

'Ruth, give me that newspaper.'

But Ruth rolled the paper up and began to slap it against her thigh.
Doing this seemed to stop her tears. She was staring out past Rebecca
through the windows shaped like diamonds to the woods behind.

'Where's Donny?' Charlie demanded. He felt strange. He could never
predict, any more, how he would react.

'With your father. Go pack. Stop, you left your sweater on the chair.
And isn't there any one you need to thank?'

Charlie's mother had a speech for him on the ride home. She said so
many families get divorced now anyway, and he saw Sarah balancing on
the cabin roof, without her sneakers, windbreaker or car keys, the
bloody sailboat in reverse, pushing, as it must have, against the bobbing
Baby Ruth.

He saw her plummet – slow motion – over the side, out of sight. Did
she tie the gun to her wrist? A brick to her leg? There were questions he
would not voice, suspicions he would not share. He saw his life stretch
out before him; unhappiness would be always creeping up. He put a
hand out for his sweater and pulled it to him, covering himself.

CRUELTY

LILA IS SITTING on her hands on the edge of the dining-room table while her parents dress upstairs. They rarely go out any more, but when they do, her father needs the extra quiet time to shower and shave. Lila's mother doesn't want anyone coming up the stairs with a load of questions.

Lila can see the backyard, which is deep and narrow and suffers from a thick canopy of neighbouring trees so that even in summer it will be cold and overcast. Although snow remains now only in patches, it is not grass that has emerged but vibrant green moss.

The phone rings and Lila hears the clip-clop of her mother's shoes as she moves over the hardwood floor in the upstairs hallway.

'Yes, hello, this is Marian.'

In the backyard stands a handsome wooden swing set Lila's father put together from a kit. A monument soaked with dampness but free of snow. He hammered his finger that day and Lila's mother ran up and down the stairs looking for Band-Aids. Her mother worries about splinters, but Lila hides them, along with the blisters, by making fists of her hands. Her mother distrusts the outdoors, in particular, backyards.

'Rick, it's for you.'

There is the whispered shuffle of Lila's father in stocking feet as he travels to the phone.

'Careful, Rick, you'll slip. That won't be good for your back.'

The maple trees are brown, and the tulip beds, the fence, the undersides of clouds. Her mother calls this another disappointing spring day in Newfoundland. Her mother is from Ontario and visits there sometimes alone, but comes back with a sad face and new clothes for everyone, saying there is no one left. A place called Kingston has become a foreign land.

Joy appears in the doorway. 'Something's going on. Listen.'

Joy is ten and does not sit on her hands while their parents dress. She sits in the kitchen and crayons.

Upstairs their mother says, her voice elevated and slightly frightened,

'You're only telling me this now?'

'No, Marian. *She* was only telling me this now. On the phone, just then.'

'Is she crazy?'

'Marian.' Their father sounds as though someone has applied glue to his tongue. Perhaps he is experimenting with a new painkiller. 'Marian, it was an innocent, kind-hearted suggestion. She has children of her own, after all. But if the baby-sitter's here, let's forget it, shall we?'

'Has she already made their supper?'

'She didn't say. Is the baby-sitter here?'

'Do you hear the baby-sitter nattering away downstairs?'

'Lila's on the table?'

'If she's already made their supper. Rick?'

'She didn't say.' Her father comes to the head of the stairs. Lila sees his navy socks. 'Lila, you can hop down now,' he calls.

Joy puts her arms out and Lila slides down into them, then stands fanning her hands, imagining them attached to the ends of her arms like two pressed leaves. In a few years she'll wait in the kitchen with Joy while their parents dress upstairs, but she doesn't think about that now.

Upstairs, there is the hollow clip-clop of their mother and more slowly, the slithering hush of their father. The room where Lila and Joy wait is growing dark. The lights are not on and neither girl has the courage to touch their mother's antique lamps. The view onto Monkstown Road is aglow. In the sky above, dozens of crows are beating their way back from the dump to Kenmount Hill where they will spend the night. Lila knows this because her father has explained it to her. He has stood at this window and counted hundreds passing overhead.

'Girls?' He is there, almost ready, his hair combed back and still wet from his shower. He'll need help with his shoes. 'How would you two like to head out with us tonight?'

'Yeah!' Joy says.

'Lila?'

Lila rushes her father, hugging him at the hips.

'Whoops,' he says, taking her by the wrists and restraining her at arm's length, gently. 'Careful of your old dad's back.'

'I've called the baby-sitter, Rick,' their mother shouts from upstairs. 'But I'm having second thoughts. Someone find your father's shoes then everyone go wait for me in the car.'

Lila's father puts a hand on Joy who, understanding the gesture, immediately pouts. 'Let your sister get them this time,' he says. 'It means a lot to her.'

'Did anyone hear me?' their mother yells.

'Yes, Marian. Loud and clear.'

'It's only common courtesy to make that acknowledgement, all of you.'

His shoes wait side by side at the back door, smelling of leather, shoe polish, pain. As she lifts them Lila has the desire to crawl inside one, down to the tips of the toes.

What Lila comes to understand on the drive over is that they are visiting a woman who works where their father did before he had to give up working. A woman with three sons, but no husband.

'I believe he went to California,' their father explains.

'California? Good Lord.'

'I believe he works as a mechanic at Disneyland. But don't quote me on that.'

'Could he get us in free?' Joy asks. 'Some kind of a deal?'

'Anything's possible.'

'Oh, Rick, don't get their hopes up like that,' their mother says with soft laughter. 'Your father's talking out of the side of his mouth. Is this it?'

They park behind two cars in a single-lane driveway. On the left is a dusty turquoise house while on the right a chain-link fence travels past the cars and up a slight incline, bordering a backyard mostly mud. Lila moves forward in her seat and sees a single tree in the middle of the yard. In the bare arms of the tree hangs a boy.

'What's that?' her mother asks.

'Back of the brewery,' Lila's father answers.

'Does it always stink this badly?'

'No idea. Come on now.'

A woman steps through the back door and waves.

'She's pretty,' Joy says.

'I guess I was thinking a little more formal,' their mother says.

Their father looks at the woman then at his wife. The woman is wearing leggings and several layers of shirts, the outermost a men's red hunting jacket. His wife is wearing a new linen skirt and her boiled wool jacket.

'Don't sweat it,' he says.

'I just wish I had known,' Lila's mother says, swiftly removing her earrings and pocketing them – a sure sign that all is lost.

Lila watches her father's jaw clench, from irritation or pain or both. He wets his lips, as though to make a fresh start. 'Come on, everybody out.'

As they move towards the house a black dog charges around the side of it, barking and leaping over invisible barrels.

The woman, who has been smiling and shifting her weight from foot to foot, possibly to stay warm, stops and puts her hands on her hips and shouts, 'How did Mackie get loose?' She seems to be addressing the boy in the tree. As though the black dog understands this it immediately heads that way, its tail batting the air unrhythmically. A German shepherd rises from the dirt at the base of the tree and yanks hard against the rope at its neck. The two dogs grapple briefly, and the black dog is off again.

'Brrr,' the women says, hugging herself as Lila and her family approach. 'So you brought the kids. Excellent. Watch out for Mackie. Down, boy!' She turns and hollers, 'Alfred!'

'I'm stuck. I can't get down,' the boy in the tree answers. He does not shout or raise his voice yet speaks with such forceful clarity he could be standing at Lila's ear.

'What a liar he is,' the woman tells Lila and Joy. She seems to find this funny. 'Alfred's after living in that tree. Mackie! Down, boy.'

The dog is avoiding the woman. Lila's father reaches for its tail, misses, and lurches awkwardly. He puts his hand on his lower back and his family stops breathing.

'Now you've done it, Rick,' their mother says. 'Do you want to go home?'

'Of course not. We only just got here.' Then he winks at the woman and jokes, 'I'm used to living with phenomenal pain.'

'Sure?' the woman asks, alarmed. Turning swiftly she seizes the dog by its neck and twists one of its ears until it slides onto its haunches at her feet and whimpers, its tail a submissive thud-thud on the wet ground. 'Oh, now, will you look at your paws. Down boy. Get down out of that!' She straightens part-way, still holding the dog, and smiles. 'How's it going, Marian?'

'I can't complain.'

'Come on in. It's freezing out here.'

'Two dogs,' Lila's mother says loudly. 'That's two more than I could handle.'

'Don't be talking! It wasn't my idea.' The woman opens the door with one hand and drags the sitting dog over the steps with her other, then puts her foot on its rear and shoves it the last distance. Lila's father and mother follow. Joy moves with her mother as though connected by a rope.

Lila doesn't budge and they disappear inside without her. She turns and stands a long time watching the boy in the tree as he climbs up one side and down the other and then back into the centre. Suspended in the branches around him are various items: a beef bucket swinging by a yellow rope, a checkered cloth bag, torn ribbons, Sobeys bags and partially deflated balloons. He's wearing a jean jacket over a grey sweatshirt with the hood snug on his head.

'Can you climb a tree or what?' he finally asks.

Lila's been waiting for this. Although she has never climbed a tree in her life and she's wearing a dress and she's cold, she runs over to the tree. The German shepherd rises like a wave.

'That thing won't hurt you. She's a big baby. Give her a pet. That's what I'd do.'

'What grade are you in?' Lila asks, hanging back.

'Grade three. I hates it.'

'I'm in grade two.'

'Sure, you don't look old enough for preschool.'

Lila has heard this before. She won't look at the boy now. She studies the dog digging at the ground with a single paw and panting so frantically its tongue skims the ground. Suddenly it barks and Lila jumps back and falls. She looks at her dress.

'Hey, don't cry,' the boy says, scrambling down through the branches. He swings from the bottom branch and lands gracefully on bent knees, his arms extended before him. He lowers his arms as his body straightens, then bows so slightly Lila nearly misses it. 'Don't go in.'

But Lila has no intention of going in. The first thing she notices about him when he squats beside her is the space between his two front teeth, which are new and not as white as the others. She says, 'It's just my dress is dirty is all. My mother will kill me.'

The boy looks away down the yard, squinting at the back of the brewery – a mustard-coloured building. He turns back and looks again at Lila's dress as though he can't quite make up his mind about it.

'What's your name anyway?'

'Lila.'

'Wanna come up in my tree?'

Lila points at the German shepherd. Alfred nods and stands, takes a few steps towards the dog then charges it, leaping onto its back and pinning himself to its neck. It whines and tosses its head.

'Hurry,' Alfred urges, though his voice is calm, almost gentle. 'I can't be holding Girlie forever.'

She gets to the tree and stops, unable to reach the bottom branch.

'See the nails?' Alfred says. 'Use 'em as steps.'

'Nails?'

'In the bark there.'

Lila has never touched a nail. She remembers her father hammering his hand, the search for a Band-Aid. Both her parents had been shouting.

'Look at the bark,' he says, still patient. 'Jesus, Girlie, you're gross. Give it up.'

Lila glances at Alfred flat on his back in the muck with the dog planted over him lapping his face. Hot gratitude rushes through her. She puts a foot on a bent nail lodged in the bark. When both feet have left the earth and she's reached the bottom branch, she hears him say, 'There you go,' and knows she'll be unhappy now for a long time because she was not born into this family.

He swings back up into the tree and joins her. 'We're too low,' he says. 'Them piranhas can still get at us.'

She follows him up to an opening where the bark is well-scarred and he can reach his things. He takes a knife out of the beef bucket and scratches something into the branch between his legs, then offers Lila use of it. She shakes her head and he tosses the knife back into the bucket, saying, 'Maybe another day then.'

He lets go with both his hands and leans back, his legs grasping the branch like hands. She wants to shout. Or touch him. His hood slips off and jacket falls open. She sees his torso tighten and his expression gain years as he grabs at the checkered cloth bag hanging from a branch behind him.

'My music bag,' he explains, sitting forward again. Inside the bag is a Sobeys bag and inside that several Oh Henry! bars. 'I'm the only kid I knows still has Halloween candy.'

She says, 'My mother won't let me go trick-or-treating.' He gives her a short satisfied nod and she knows she has said the right thing.

Cars are pulling up and people getting out and coming up to the house. Lila watches her own car become blocked in. The people wave at Alfred and Lila in the tree as they pass, but Alfred ignores them. 'Jerks,' he mumbles, his mouth full of candy bar. He's fishing around inside his pants, scratching himself and grimacing. He pushes his pants down and handles a small nubby object that seems to be irritating him. He slaps it.

He looks at her and smiles. 'Just my old penis breath.' He shoves it back into his pants, then slaps his zipper.

'Who were all those people?' Lila asks.

'Jerks. Have you ever been to Disneyland?'

She grins. 'I know.'

'What do you know?' He sounds cross.

'Your father has a job there.'

'And that I visits there whenever I wants?'

She's hoping he'll invite her. She's hoping so hard, she doesn't notice him lean over and take hold of a strand of her hair. He yanks it out.

'Did that hurt?' he asks.

'No.'

'It was hanging in your face.'

'I wonder if it's time for supper?' she whispers.

'Sure, could be finished by now. Were you expecting someone to call you in? Gotta just go. Hold it.' He raises a hand and pauses, waiting until satisfied that he has her full attention. 'Girlie's not asleep yet, I wouldn't make no move. You got another loose hair. Did that hurt?'

'No.'

The next Saturday Lila is playing in her bedroom when her mother comes in and says, 'That was Alfred's mother on the phone. Remember the little boy you got so dirty with? He wants you to visit him this afternoon.' Her mother scrunches up her face. 'That's not really something you want to do, is it?'

Lila has been thinking about Alfred and his tree all week. 'Oh, Mommy, yes, please!'

'Let her make up her own mind, Marian,' Lila's father says from somewhere.

Her mother frowns. 'All right. But I'm going to put out pants and a wool sweater for you. Their house was freezing. And wet.'

'Why was it wet?' Lila asks.

'Shame you never uttered more than two sentences, Marian,' Lila's father calls.

'Because she had just washed the floor! There were puddles, in fact. I took off my shoes to be polite and then my feet got wet and I froze. I don't think they had the heat on, quite frankly.'

'Marian.'

'Yeah, yeah, yeah. I'm just explaining why she needs to dress warmly. And don't remove your shoes inside their house.'

'We'll probably play outside,' Lila says carefully.

'No climbing trees,' her father says.

'Where are you, Rick?'

'I'm resting my back.'

'Of course no climbing trees, Lila, that goes without saying. Children are forever falling out of trees and breaking their arms.'

Her mother walks to the doorway and looks down the hall. 'Is that comfortable?' she asks him.

'Nothing's comfortable.'

That afternoon while Lila is at Alfred's her father checks himself into the Health Sciences. He drives over himself without change for the meter or telling anyone, then calls just before supper, medicated and humble.

Lila's mother drops the supper plates before the girls, hurls the pots and pans into the sink, the leftovers into the refrigerator. Everything she touches she seems to hate.

'Are you mad at me?' Joy whines.

'No, treasure. Your father. He's set on doing everything his own way.

Again. Now I'm going over to that hospital and we'll have two cars collecting tickets. I mean, why didn't he just ask me for a lift?'

'You're going to the hospital?' Joy asks.

'Well, I think I better. They might operate.' For a moment her voice lightens, as though she's amused by the idea of not rushing to her husband's side. 'Although, frankly, this place. The medical care. It takes forever to get anything done. I mean, a simple X-ray?'

Lila puts a finger into each of her ears. But she can still hear the crying Joy will begin any moment.

'I could have dropped him off this afternoon then picked you up at that boy's house,' she says to Lila. 'It was right on the way.' She slams the refrigerator door and on top of it the ceramic bowl of apples bounces towards the edge. 'No, he has to do everything his own way. Now settle down, both of you.'

The phone rings. It's sitting right there in the middle of the table and they all jump. Joy and her mother both reach for it but Joy is quicker.

'Just give it to me,' their mother hisses.

Joy hands the phone to her mother who immediately tries to interrupt. 'If I could just …' she begins, then stops, her head thrust forward with the air of someone struggling with the incomprehensible. She looks so annoyed Lila thinks she might bite the receiver. 'Sometime, perhaps. Can I get back to you on this?' She hangs up and looks at Lila curiously. 'So you know about this? You want to have a sleepover at that boy's house? That woman is really getting on my nerves. From the moment your father tried to collar that mutt of hers he's been paying for it. Of course they'll never operate. Not after three operations already. Nobody'll touch him.'

Alfred has long lashes and black hair that his mother trims with the scissors on her jackknife. She also uses the jackknife to open cans of tuna fish and tomato soup. Lila is fascinated by the speed at which her hand circles the can.

Today Alfred showed her his rocks. He keeps them on a wooden shelf on his bedroom wall. Lila didn't think much of the collection at first, the rocks were so dirty and crumbling. She would have expected a fleck or two of silver or gold, this being Alfred who has been to Disneyland. The game they played with the rocks involved putting a bunch in their socks and underwear and down the backs of their shirts, then going out into the tree. Alfred took a while selecting hers.

As they approached the tree Alfred tackled Girlie, again urging Lila to hurry. She scrambled up through the branches despite the rocks under her feet and between her legs, so thrilled when Alfred praised her that it was easy to make peace with her pain. As it was later, when he plucked out her hair or took her hand and bent it forward at the wrist until the tips of her cold pink fingers brushed her coat sleeve.

'Does this hurt?'

'No.'

'Does this?'

'No.'

'You got a gift there, girl.'

She looked away, afraid he'd see her happiness. It came to her naturally, this gift.

Her father returned from the hospital unopened, grey and muted, with a new prescription that made him feel so stupid he tossed it out within a day.

Lila's mother's enthusiasm for housework immediately began to wane; she roamed the house glum and short-tempered until at last she decided to make a visit back to Ontario.

She stood at the door with her bags and said, 'I've just got to get out of here, Rick.'

'I understand.'

'I'm not trying to punish you.'

'Have a good time now. Enjoy yourself.'

'I don't know why I'm going. I can't relate to any of those people any more.'

'Go on. Don't worry about a thing.'

'Yeah, yeah, yeah. Oh, look at your poor daughter.'

Joy was coming down the hallway, sobbing.

'I'm counting on you and Lila to help your father. Don't hang off me, treasure.'

Lila was sitting at the top of the stairs. She wouldn't come down. It was always a little scary when their mother left, shucking her role as though the antique lamps and polished floors, the sweet-smelling sheets and nicely dressed daughters had never meant anything to her.

Although the last thing in the world they did was help their father. He shuffled around the house in his pyjamas, ordered Chinese food and pizzas and let the house get turned upside down. It was understood that their mother expected to come home to a frenzy of domestic chores.

With her mother away Lila began to visit Alfred more often. She rarely saw his brothers, but his mother would be there, the cordless tucked under an ear as she patrolled the house busy at some new project, the most recent being the washing of all the windows with vinegar and newspapers. She'd laugh and nod and carry on, and gradually the house bloomed with an acidic odour that clung to Lila's clothes long after she was home again, a reminder of that foreign world that was her secret.

Alfred's mother had relaxed rules about food, and without argument allowed them to carry off whole bags of Mr Christie's Favorites or Raspberry Temptations. Perched beside Alfred in the tree, Lila could only eat two or three – the smell of the brewery so close it was as though it were routing its way through her own bloodstream and slowly escaping her lungs, but Alfred could always finish the bag. Occasionally he dropped one onto Girlie, who would be moving around on her belly in the muck below, her yellow eyes turned up to them with longing.

'You and me,' Alfred said one day, removing a rusty wire dog brush from his jean jacket. 'We could get married.'

'Soon?' She held her breath.

'No. What are you saying?' He pinched her. 'When we're grown up. Pinky swear?' He offered her his little finger, crooked like the letter C, and she put her own into it.

That night Lila dreamed that she and Alfred had climbed high into his tree. Overhead the crows were going home to roost, calling out in unnatural voices that reminded her of her father's electric razor. The sound racked the tree, convulsing the branches and scaring Lila, so Alfred set to wrapping her in bedclothes that smelled of flat Coke and mown grass but were as soft as anything and radiated heat. She had been so cold before. Then he tied his rope around her waist and lowered her, face first, towards the earth.

She dropped over Girlie, who whined, the sound of it echoing off the back of the brewery, which had moved so near the tree Lila could see where the last coat of paint did not quite cover the first. Then Girlie opened her mouth and without warning her face was transformed into the face of Lila's father, staring up at her with shining yellow eyes.

* * *

It had been sunny all day. In fact, it had been sunny two days running and in the morning Lila's mother had opened a window to admire the daffodils that had emerged, slightly crooked, in the back yard. She stood there, inhaling deeply, bestowing upon this view such a rare generous smile that everyone felt they deserved to be happy. After that she spent several hours going up and down the stairs, humming 'I'll Be Home for Christmas', cleaning house and fetching things for Lila's father who moved from room to room, floor to floor, looking for comfort.

Lila had been to Alfred's in the morning. When she got home she changed into her nightgown and got into bed and lay facing the ceiling, her hands tucked fast beneath the small of her back. Her body hurt from the rocks and the dog brush. Her scalp seemed to belong to someone else.

'Lila?' Her mother came into her room with an armload of dirty laundry. 'Did they give you lunch?'

Lila nodded. 'She can make six sandwiches out of one can of tuna fish.'

'Like I'm surprised. Why are you in bed?' Her mother moved across the room gathering up Lila's clothes at great speed. After a while she let everything drop back to the floor except for Lila's underwear, which she shook timidly, and together Lila and her mother watched the broken rocks fall to the carpet.

She had to call Lila's father several times and when he appeared he looked sad and his body thoroughly askew. Lila's mother showed him the underwear, and at once the two of them began glancing at each other then back at the underwear like a couple of hens, until he took it in his hands and looked as though he might lift it to his nose, but Lila's mother said sharply, 'Rick!' and he stopped.

Lila watched her parents. It was like stepping into another world to see the skill with which they could suddenly communicate.

'Dear,' her father began casually, but Lila wasn't fooled. 'Who took your clothes off?'

'No one did.'

'You did?'

'No.'

'Treasure, they have dirt in them.'

'I put rocks in them. And in my socks. And down the back of my blouse. I did it.'

'Could you tell us why?'

'It's Alfred's game he taught me.'

'Just Alfred?'

'Yes.'

'But why did you put rocks in your underwear?'

'To protect me.'

'From what?'

'Alfred, see, he's worried about piranhas. But I liked the way it felt. I liked the pain.'

Her father stepped back to rest against the wall. Her mother folded up the underwear. Both seemed to have become less interested and Lila was in agony that they would leave the room. They didn't understand.

'Pain,' her father said. 'Christ almighty. Why would anyone want pain?'

'I do. I want to live with it. It's like ...' She lowered her voice, wanting only her father to hear. 'It's like I want to marry it.'

'What are you saying?'

'That's all you were doing?' her mother said. 'Putting rocks in your underwear? This is just a little too peculiar for me, Rick. I don't want her over there.'

'Neither do I.'

'I hope you realize this is your fault.'

'Give me a break, woman.'

'But, Daddy, you live with pain.'

'Not by choice, I sure as hell don't.'

She had expected admiration, reward, a tight hug. 'But, Daddy.'

'I didn't choose this life! Do you understand me?' He was angry. When he was angry, he hurt more. 'Does everyone understand me?' he shouted.

Although her father rarely raised his voice, Lila was not surprised, but it exacerbated her cuts and bruises so that her skin seemed to leap from her bones. She closed her eyes. She thought of asking them to leave if they couldn't be quiet.

'You could try another doctor,' her mother said, angry in her own way, which was more knife-like and brittle. 'You could try another province. Or maybe you like hanging around this house year after year making us all miserable with your bellyaching.'

'You just have no idea, do you?' And as he spoke he travelled across the room, gritting his teeth because he was having such a bad day, and shoved Lila's mother against the bedroom wall.

Lila's voice was raspy, as though her throat had been injured in some way, but her shouting served to draw her father off her mother and back to her. As he came towards her, his misery and rage shining, Lila realized that this was the father she had been a long time expecting: the man inside the man who without complaint stooped crookedly at the back door to remove his shoes, rose slowly from a bed, or cleared the corner in the upstairs hall in his stocking feet just seconds ahead of disaster.

FRANK AND AGNES

'YOU REMEMBER that habit of hers. When she was five, six, seven?' Frank said to Agnes. 'It's no surprise, considering that, what she's doing now.'

'No.'

'Yes, you do, Agnes.'

'Search me.'

'I have to spell it out, do I?'

'I guess so.' Agnes leaned forward in the bed and reached behind her to better prop herself with the pillows. She was laughing.

'That summer she went without underwear. Agnes!'

'Oh, Frank. What are you talking about?'

'I believe there was a tendency in her then, even at that age.'

'A tendency, Frank? A tendency towards what?'

He disappeared into the bathroom, came out again in his pyjamas and said, 'Promiscuity.'

'Stop it.' She watched him circle the room and return to her. 'Those summers were the best days of my life,' she said.

'You sound like her.'

'Should I mind that? You sound like I should mind that. She's my daughter. People get divorced.'

'Adultery? I am well aware the word's passé, Agnes. Nevertheless ...' But Agnes looked so angry he stopped. He sat down on the edge of the bed. After a while he said, 'I'm losing my mind.'

'Underwear,' she told him, addressing his bowed back.

'Right! And I still think I'm on to something. Those Fridays I'd come out here and invariably she'd be waltzing around in those soiled dresses –'

'All that sewing I used to do ...'

'– without underwear!'

'You came out Saturday mornings.'

'I did not. I got off work and beat it up here for the last ferry.'

'Maybe the first year.'

'Okay,' he said.

'Never mind, Frank. But I really can't remember her going without underwear.'

'I'd step off that ferry and she'd be hanging off the railings there – where children were prohibited, by the way – and she'd climb her feet up the sides, her dress would fall back, and there were her privates. Certainly there are *some* things we don't need to see.'

'You should have said something.'

He shrugged. 'Embarrassed, I suppose.'

'I'm sure it wasn't intentional, or genetically driven, as you seem to be suggesting. She was always in such a rush to run off with her friends, or meet you at the ferry, that she forgot to put some on.'

'I honestly don't know the answer to that.'

'It wasn't a question, Frank.'

'And now she's getting divorced.'

'Yes.'

'And ...'

'Whatever you want to call.'

'Carrying on?'

'Yes,' she said.

After a few fitful twists and turns in bed, Frank was asleep. All this happening, and he was finding it easy to sleep. Agnes did not find it easy. She was too hot, for one thing. Here it was fall but the cool temperatures were slow coming. The bedroom windows were open, yet there was something about the dark out there this time of year that frightened her; after an hour or so she usually accepted the heat and closed the windows. There was no longer that buoyant summer promise, the feeling that during the night as you slept wonderful secret things were happening outside, so that when you awoke in the morning all those night-time noises – the buzzes, the clicks, and in the last hours, the singing – paid off in the deliverance of a shimmering day.

Now when she thought of the outside she thought of decaying flower beds and a shredded hedge, and everywhere the colours feeble and drained, and something else – huddled and cold, a child's bogeyman.

Agnes refused to blame herself for the current state of Julie's life, nor would she interfere. In fact, if it weren't for those three children without any notion of the word restraint – despite Julie's constant battling with them – it might do Julie and Raymond some good to spend time apart.

It was only weeks ago, the middle of August, when Raymond had talked them into going to the Blue Jay for lunch. Frank had been worn out from getting the new screens in and the ride over that unpaved road to the other end of the island could seem endless. And Raymond had invited every neighbourhood child he'd laid eyes on; he and Julie had that cursed van.

The Blue Jay had not existed when Agnes's children were small. It was a little blue building surrounded by massive oaks and a wooden patio for eating. There was a window where you ordered and paid, then off you went to claim your table and wait an unfathomably long time with the hornets before they called you by your first name to come get your food, which was overpriced and tasteless.

'This place is such a rip-off,' Simon said. Simon was fifteen, the oldest.

'I'll tell you what, Simon,' Julie said. 'You can help pay for lunch with that attitude and this week's allowance. How's that?'

But Agnes knew Julie would never keep to this. By the end of the day, guilt and second thoughts would get to her.

It was crowded, as Frank had predicted, and the adults – along with Simon – found a place in the shade while the younger children went straight for the empty tables out on the hot lawn.

Agnes sat down, hoping they could sort out the ordering without her. 'I'll have a lobster roll and iced tea, dear,' she told Frank.

'Shall I make sure they put in some ice for you?'

'Please.'

'Ice. I'm sure it's just a bunch of kids running this place. Ice. You'd think it would be included automatically.' But Frank didn't move. Agnes knew he wasn't comfortable with this business of going to them to place his order; he'd rather they came to him, pad of paper in hand.

'Even Simon could run this place,' Frank muttered.

Agnes glanced at her grandson but he hadn't heard. He and Julie were still bickering over his allowance.

'Where's Dad?' Simon asked.

'Don't think you'll get anything out of him,' Julie told her son. 'If he gives you one penny he can walk home.'

'I hate you, Mom,' Simon said softly.

'Well, I hate you too, honey.'

Agnes disregarded this exchange, she had found it was the best approach, and Frank, she saw, had not heard. He was still standing there, staring across at the little window.

'Go help your father order, Julie,' Agnes said. 'So Raymond's gone off. It won't prevent the kids from getting hungry.' The place was crowded and noisy, but already Agnes had heard the voices of her two other grandchildren, Timothy and Emma, crescendo above all other sounds.

Frank and Julie came back with the drinks – thick with ice – which they distributed to everyone. Intermittent shouts and screams on the lawn made their way over to the adults, but it wasn't until one voice rose clearly above the rest, 'Mom, Emma said *fuck!*' that Julie pushed back her chair with that stony look of hers and went over to make – Agnes had no doubt – a number of threats.

At last the food was ready and Agnes helped Julie distribute the hamburgers and fries to the children.

All of the hamburgers had mayonnaise. It was apparently unexpected. One very thin boy – Agnes had never seen him before – turned a disappointed face to Julie and pointed to his hamburger where a smear of mayonnaise was turning transparent in the heat. 'Oh, for Christ's sake,' Julie began, then stopped, put a hand on the boy's shoulder and said, 'Go get a knife to scrape it off, Rusty.'

Timothy pushed his meal away and said to his mother in that end-of-the-world tone of his, 'There's no *way* I'm gonna eat that.'

'You look flushed, sweetheart,' Agnes said to Emma. 'Why don't you come sit with the grown-ups under the trees?'

'That's a good idea,' Julie said. 'I meant to separate you two.'

Emma followed them back to the patio, but when Simon wouldn't move so she could sit beside her mother, she refused to touch her meal.

'Emmie's a little baby. Has to sit next to her mommy,' Simon said.

After that Emma kept slipping away, back to the boys' table, and Julie kept going over to retrieve her. Each time Emma returned she had more and more catsup on her shirt, and was looking so hot Agnes was afraid she'd get sunstroke. Then they heard Timothy shout, 'Mom, Emma put catsup on Rusty's hat. Mom! Aren't you going to punish her?'

'Where *is* Raymond?' Agnes asked Frank. Although he never said a word, Frank was usually uncomfortable with this public scene-making. Today, however, he seemed unconscious of it. Agnes thought it might be time to have his hearing checked again.

She watched Emma trail Julie back across the lawn, then suddenly throw herself down on the grass. Julie turned and said, 'Get up, Emma.'

But you couldn't blame Julie, Agnes thought. Raymond was always up to this: taking them somewhere and disappearing. Right now he was probably having a drink in someone's kitchen, not far away. He might even be watching them.

Agnes sipped her iced tea. There was so much ice it was finished already. She watched as Julie sat down on the grass beside Emma, who was so angry she looked unwell. Despite the heat her face was white and those brown eyes appeared to be moving inwards, closer together.

When Emma gave her brother and his friends the finger, using both hands, Agnes almost laughed. It was not a practised gesture: her fingers were gathered beneath each thumb so that her middle fingers stuck out awkwardly from round little fists. She kept jabbing the air with these fists, looking so inexperienced, and suddenly, seeing those two – mother and daughter – struggling to get through the afternoon, Agnes felt old.

Timothy began yelling, 'Look! She's giving us the finger! Mom, aren't you going to punish her for that? *Oh my God*, I can't believe it, you're not going to punish her!' Just in case, Agnes thought, there was anyone here for lunch not yet aware of their family.

Then, miraculously, mother and daughter stood and began walking away.

'Why are you holding her hand?' Timothy shrieked. 'Isn't she in trouble?'

Emma was crying now, clinging to her mother and stumbling along. Agnes watched them, God knew when they'd be back. She turned to Frank, who winked at her and said, 'Well, Miss America, I guess it's up to you and me to hold down the fort now,' and she looked away, embarrassed by her relief.

Agnes kicked away the sheets. When she couldn't sleep at night her calves felt so tense, and her feet so hot, it was all she could do to stay still.

She'd like to roll around the bed, fling her legs from one side to the other, somehow get this edginess out of her.

Frank hadn't stirred, thank goodness. He lay on his side with the summer blanket pulled up over his shoulders. All their married life he had run cold and she had run hot, and nothing had changed as they'd grown older. Frank would rise early, as he always did, and she would sleep the morning hours away, catching up.

She couldn't remember whether she'd shut the windows. She hated this getting up again and again in the night to fool with the windows, the sheets, the door. If the windows were open it was a good idea to shut the door or at least lodge it open with a pillow, since a breeze could come up and rattle the door just as you were finally dozing off. Of course what was worse was waking and not being sure which bed you were in. Which house. Here on the island the bed faced the windows; in the city there was only that small one on Frank's side. But just last week she had awoken and expected the windows to be behind her, which had been unnerving – it was years since their bed had been on that side of the room.

Underwear? Agnes couldn't remember. When she searched for an image of Julie at that age she saw Emma, slumped murderous and neglected on the lawn at the Blue Jay. What a day. Once they were home, she had reminded everyone that the Bartletts were expected for drinks at five. Julie had groaned. Frank went for a nap, and Raymond for the Glenfiddich.

Joe and Lucy Bartlett brought along their granddaughter Melissa, who was staying with them. Raymond, who hadn't showered or changed, took the chair across from Melissa and Mrs Bartlett and began suggesting various cocktails, all of which Melissa refused, blushing.

'I've been trying to get your granny to run off with me for years,' Raymond told Melissa. It was so absurd neither Melissa nor Mrs Bartlett bothered to suppress a smile. Agnes stood by with a plate of cheese and crackers.

He leaned forward. 'So, how about me and you run off for the weekend?' He looked at Mrs Bartlett. 'What's her name again?'

'Melissa,' Melissa said.

Julie arrived with drinks. 'A G&T for you, Mrs Bartlett and –'

'What are you giving her? Not fruit juice!'

He sounded so crestfallen Mrs Bartlett glanced at her granddaughter, but Agnes smiled and said, 'Don't pay any attention to Raymond. We don't.'

'Get up,' Julie said to Raymond. She was kicking his feet. 'Go show Mr Bartlett your new skiff. He'd love to see it. And take Daddy.'

'Yes,' Mrs Bartlett agreed.

But Frank and Joe returned within minutes; Raymond was going to take the skiff out for a run-around on his own.

'Aren't you worried about him out on the water all by himself?' Melissa asked, addressing both Julie and Agnes, and the question, so guileless, took them by surprise.

When Raymond returned from his boat ride, Agnes hoped he'd behave himself, but he couldn't stay seated and kept bouncing up to pace around the room. He stopped in front of Melissa and said, 'Come on, have a drink.'

'Leave her alone, Raymond.'

'I can't,' Melissa said. 'I have to get up early. I'm taking the first ferry in the morning. Now stop bothering me,' she added, a little breathlessly.

'Excuse me, Raymond,' Mrs Bartlett said. She was trying to stand but Raymond blocked her way, as well as, Agnes noted, her view of her husband, who was discussing with Frank plans to replace the electric cable to the island. At last Mrs Bartlett rose, but not before Raymond nearly sat on her lap in his hurry to claim her seat beside Melissa, who frowned at him.

'You can have a drink and still get up early,' he said. 'Frank does it every day.' Now that he was close to her – as close as he'd ever get – he relaxed. Agnes glanced at her watch.

Frank broke off his discussion with Mr Bartlett to look over at Raymond. 'Did you say something to me, Raymond?'

'Yes, sir. Frank has a drink and still gets up early. Four o'clock. I really admire him. Oh, you should hear him. *I got up at four and did this and this and this.* Then he takes a nap. Agnes over there gets up at the crack of eleven, then makes her way downstairs like a blind woman for her coffee and bran flakes. She's not ready for the world until about one, when she has to do something about that head, as Frank refers to her hair.'

'I'm sorry, Melissa,' Julie apologized, though Agnes thought it was unnecessary – Melissa had laughed out loud during Raymond's sketch of their personal life. 'He always does this. He always ruins everything. He thinks he's funny, but he's not, is he? Raymond, Melissa doesn't think you're funny for a minute.'

'No, I really don't.'

Now she was flirting. It was inevitable.

'Were you watching me out there, dear?' he asked her.

'Out where?'

'In the skiff.'

'No. Not really.'

'But I was showing off for you!'

'You don't have to shout everything, Raymond.'

Mrs Bartlett had returned from the bathroom and was sitting down beside Julie. 'We're used to Raymond, you know that, Julie. Nothing he says seems unusual. Do you still have that platter we gave you?'

'Mrs Bartlett, that platter is so practical. It's our favourite wedding present.'

'And how are the children?'

'Oh, really great.' Julie managed a smile and looked at the floor. Agnes saw that the moment of willing away everything you own and love for the chance to strangle your husband had passed. It occurred to her how mistaken Frank was to think Julie's recent behaviour was about anything more than staying, or not staying, in a marriage.

'You mean way out there?' Melissa asked Raymond, pointing to the inlet through the sliding glass doors. 'I wouldn't be able to see you way out there. I'd need binoculars or a telescope or something.'

But Raymond's interest in Melissa was winding down; he had been following Julie's conversation with Mrs Bartlett. 'Our favourite wedding present?' he wondered, looking at his wife, then added, 'The binoculars are missing in action.'

'What did you say?' Melissa asked.

'I think they finally took them away from Frank.'

The Bartletts left soon after that. But before they did, Agnes had the experience of being made privy to all the years of gossip ever said about you. Whoosh. Now you knew.

Frank and his binoculars.

But the binoculars had not been taken away; Frank had misplaced them early in the summer and with that vague, befuddled air that had recently come to him, orbited away from his old habits without, it appeared to Agnes, a care in the world.

It was the look on Lucy's face she took pains not to wear, and the glance she was careful not to exchange with Joe, that told Agnes everything. For years, Frank had been watching people, people he knew, people doing absolutely nothing of any consequence, and they had all known. It was a pastime, a hobby. Frank was nosy. There were worse things.

He watched from the window over the kitchen sink, from the sliding glass doors in the living room, and most blatantly, she supposed, from his boathouse. He knew who was back on the island, who had just shopped for groceries or returned from golf, who went to bed early and who was faithful to their gardens. And all their married life he had reported these discoveries to her, and she had accepted each like a gift, knowing that somehow, by keeping an eye on everyone, he was protecting her.

But did he know other things? Did he know who had visits from police in the night, who slammed their doors and kicked their dogs, who was really loved, and by whom?

What Agnes realized just before the Bartletts said their goodnights was that not only had people known they were being watched – my God, she and Frank had been coming to the island for forty years – but that they had not liked it. There was something wrong with a man, they must have said a dozen times, who was such a snoop he spent the good part of his day spying on you with a pair of binoculars.

When Agnes awoke again it was finally morning and Frank was still asleep beside her. She was surprised to see the windows were open. She must have reopened them in the night, though she had only the faintest memory of doing so.

In the kitchen she brewed her coffee. The window above the sink was also open, which was unusual, and the air coming in was cool, carrying with it the smell of the sea and a smell that Agnes could only describe as *fallish*. The whole kitchen smelled *fallish*.

She tidied around the sink, throwing out some nasty-looking dill that had been propped in a glass of water to freshen over a week ago, then sponged away the black gunk around the faucets that Frank was oblivious to. Frank was usually the first up and about, as Raymond had pointed out to Melissa; it was years since Agnes had the silent morning kitchen to herself. She was thinking about Julie's insufficient dress code as a child, how this was a thing Frank had kept from her, something that would surely have embarrassed her back then, when she turned to glance at the wall clock behind her and saw that it was ten-thirty.

'Ten-thirty already,' she said out loud, surprised again by the cool air that had entered the house in the night.

REUNION

I SQUIRMED in the back seat, the 1975 high school yearbook open on my knees. The evening heat was syrupy and unfamiliar. I studied the back of Jane's tidy perm, but she was as impassive as always, untouched by temperature, while Winnie, who had gained considerable weight since high school, seemed to relish the sticky air. Although there was a brush of moisture along her hairline and her blue checkered dress pinched her tightly at the armpits, she was settled behind the wheel as though she had grown there, occupying that small space in the world as would a luxurious plant.

I was astonished by their matter-of-fact manner, their apparent lack of self-loathing; surely they were having second thoughts, as I was, en route to our twentieth high school reunion?

'I wish I wasn't here.'

Jane turned and looked at me steadily, frowning. 'You need to come out of the north more often, Yvonne,' she declared. For two decades, *the north* had been Jane's way of referring to my home in Canada.

'No, what she needs is a drink,' Winnie said. 'Or a smoke,' she added, rummaging through her handbag until she shook out a needle-thin joint, which she held aloft.

'That would destroy me,' I said, peeved. Winnie didn't know me at all.

'How about one of these?' Jane asked, producing a roll of sugar-free breath-savers. Jane had grown so thin in anticipation of this event she nearly rattled. I thought enviously of her two children at home not far from here, rapt before the television.

I was suddenly annoyed with the extremes of both these women. They seemed to leave me in a no man's land of average weight and identity. And now they wanted to get me high and freshen my breath.

'I'd only think about Rudy, if I smoked that,' I said.

There was a short silence before Jane asked, 'How is he?'

'He's fine. He could be dead.'

Jane turned and looked me over. 'You look great.'

'Sure,' I said, because great was not how I looked. The dress I wore was an old Indian print, faded and tawdry; it could easily have passed for something salvaged from high school days. I picked up the yearbook and began to flip through it. Twenty years ago the three of us had been as satiny and resolute as marble, but unfinished, barely distinguishable from one another.

'Here's Teddy Lawson,' I said, my finger pressed over the face of a boy with fine yellow hair scraggly on his neck in the fashion of the mid-seventies. 'You know what he did to me in fifth grade? He stuck his finger in my ass.'

Winnie gagged on her breath-saver and Jane's head shook as she laughed silently, which comforted me; sometimes it was hard to get a laugh out of Jane.

Winnie pounded her chest. 'There's a nice walk down memory lane.'

Jane handed the flask to me, insisting, 'You really do look great.' I stared at her until I understood.

'You too, Jane.'

'Well —'

'I thought Teddy Lawson went to prep school,' I said, looking back down at a boy the memory of whom I had managed to keep with me for over twenty years.

'You're right, he did,' Jane said.

'So what's he doing in our graduating class?'

'Who was Teddy Lawson?'

'Winnie, you never remember anything,' Jane said. 'Ted Lawson's mother was from Denmark or Florida or somewhere. She lived in her bikini in one of the houses on the point. His father was not so nice.'

'A mean bastard,' suggested Winnie, who knew nothing about it.

'I'm not surprised he stuck his hand up Yvonne,' Jane said and we laughed again.

'Show me his photo,' Winnie demanded and I leaned over the seat with the book. 'Looks harmless.'

'Apparently not to Yvonne,' Jane said.

'It was fifth grade,' I reminded them.

Winnie turned into the parking lot. We sat in the dark with the windows up, despite the heat, and sipped on the flask. Cars were pulling in and couples getting out. We didn't recognize anyone.

'Are we the only ones without our spouses?' Winnie asked.

Jane sighed. 'Makes you wonder.'

'It never occurred to me,' I said.

'Me either,' Winnie said.

'Though someone had to stay home with Rudy,' I added, but I said this gently because I no longer wanted to make this evening a failure.

'Let's go in,' Jane said.

Inside the club the air was cold, the air conditioning presumably on bust. There was only a scattering of fluorescent lights overhead; it took me a moment to make out the swarms of unfamiliar faces. There was a bar at the far end and against one wall several tables had been pushed. Winnie and I took a seat while Jane bought drinks.

'You can't sit,' Jane whispered when she returned. 'You're being ignored.'

She was right. There were few people sitting. Most were standing, mingling, catching up, and no one was approaching our table.

'I'm not standing,' Winnie said loudly. 'Not until they bring out some food.'

I looked around. More than half the men were bald, paunchy; they seemed to have fared significantly less well than the women, the majority of whom wore spare dresses that nicely revealed tanned athletic limbs. I was willing to bet that most of these women weighed less now than they had twenty years ago. With the exception of Winnie, of course, but also of me.

'This is a nightmare,' I said, and Jane gave me one of her looks as she rose, promising, 'I'll be right back.'

'This isn't so bad, Yvonne,' Winnie assured me. 'Who are all these people, anyway?'

'I hated high school,' I said. 'I hated everyone, everyone hated me.'

Winnie laughed. 'What about me and Jane?'

I stared at Winnie. 'You and I weren't friends.'

She stared back. 'I thought we were.'

'No, Winnie we were not,' I told her, too overcome by my desire to flee to remind her that for the most part our relationship had been one of competition for Jane.

'I thought we hung out together,' Winnie said.

I was smiling at her, trying to think of something to say, when I noticed a man moving rapidly towards me. He slid across the floor and landed kneeling at my side. 'Yvonne,' he said.

I glanced at Winnie but she shrugged massively. The man had tea-brown hair cut in a military style and his skin had a peeled-away look, scabrous with the remains of either bad acne or some kind of combat involving small knives. I looked down where his open collar revealed the upper reaches of what must have been quite a nest of chest hair. I thought of Jane's expression, *coming out of the north*, and felt unequal to the chit-chat required of me.

I shook my head apologetically. I didn't know him.

'Teddy Lawson,' he said, less breezily, but putting his hand out for mine.

'Did you graduate with us?' I asked, puzzled; despite the clear evidence in the yearbook that he had attended graduation, I still believed Teddy Lawson had gone away to school.

He gave me a stern look. In that moment before he stood and walked away, I realized I had made a mistake.

'That's not Teddy Lawson,' I tried to tell Winnie, who was laughing at me. 'Look how long his legs are!'

'He grew.'

'I thought he was sent to prep school,' I persisted. 'Where's Jane?'

'She's mingling.'

I glanced around. Winnie and I were the only people in the entire room sitting. 'Listen, Winnie,' I said. 'We have to get up. We have to talk to people, we can't just sit here.'

'Why do we have to talk to people?'

I turned away from her and scanned the room and spotted Teddy Lawson surrounded by old buddies. He waved.

'Christ.'

Jane returned with fresh drinks and the class scrapbook tucked under her arm. 'Tequila sunrises!' she cried and almost missed her seat. 'What did you say to Ted Lawson? He's going around telling everyone Yvonne Dearborn doesn't know who he is.'

'Yvonne,' Winnie said to me, opening the scrapbook. 'You don't mean he actually put his finger into your ...?'

'Yes, I do,' I said primly. 'We were walking down the hall, changing classes. I was wearing my fake leather jumper and red fish-net stockings and he was behind me.'

'You had a fake leather jumper in fifth grade?' Jane asked. 'You mean one of those plastic dresses? I don't remember that.'

'Listen,' I said. 'I was very upset. It was a strange thing for him to do.'

'No kidding it was a strange thing,' Winnie howled, then added, 'Here he is, Yvonne.' She began reading from the scrapbook. 'Career marine. Home: Texas. Married. Eight children, four adopted. That's a nice bundle.'

She slid the book across the table. There he was in a recent snapshot taken at an amusement park. I counted eight children. Four were of Asian descent. His wife was blond and short – very short. Teddy was standing heads above them all, staring straight into the camera, his expression one of pride and honour.

'Oh barf.' I stood. 'Who wants what?'

Jane said, 'Get me a pack of cigarettes.'

But halfway across the room to the bar, I was intercepted by Teddy Lawson. He pointed a cigar at me and said, stooping, 'Sorry for walking away on you, Yvonne. But I was a little hurt you didn't know me.'

'I do know you. I just thought you went to prep school.'

'That's right! Grades six through nine I went to Bellingham Academy. My parents were divorcing and it was rough at home. But I came back in tenth grade.'

'Well, that explains it,' I said, making a move to the bar.

'Yes.'

But we both knew it didn't entirely. What I knew, simply, was that I had gone through high school with blinders on. Though the blinders were off now, I was still unable to make sense of what I saw. I looked around at the people my classmates had become. Who had I become?

'Yvonne.' Teddy Lawson put a hand on my shoulder. 'Do you remember the field trip to see *2001* in fifth grade?'

'Yes.'

'Do you remember, I sat next to you?'

I stood, blinking from his cigar smoke. I had no recollection of anyone sitting beside me. What's more, I probably had no idea who was sitting beside me even at the time. Yet, this is was what he remembered? This only?

'I guess I was sort of sweet on you,' he told me.

It was a confession. I listened as he summarized his life, and gradually began to hate him and direct towards him all my anger of the past three years. I blamed him for everything, knowing he was not to blame.

'You have children?' he asked.

'One son.' And in my mind's eyes I saw Rudy at two, a roly-poly toddler at the back steps, picking wet leaves from the sides of his sneakers.

'How old?' Teddy asked.

'He's five now.'

'That's a great age. Kindergarten, right?'

He was clearly an involved father. I burst out with an ugly noise – part giggle, part cry, and put my hand to my mouth. It occurred to me that the only way out of this conversation was by asking him what the hell he thought he was doing ramming his finger into my bottom in fifth grade, but he had pinned me with an earnest, level look and I realized I was stuck in no man's land again.

'He had meningitis two years ago,' I explained. 'So we're keeping him back a year. He's deaf. He's lucky.'

Teddy was hunched over me, nodding.

'I don't know if you can imagine it,' I said suddenly, still blaming him.

'I can imagine it.'

'You want your child back no matter what. At any cost.'

'Whatever remains of him,' Teddy Lawson said.

'Yes.'

'Like a war.'

'Exactly.' And I saw my spongy-skinned, bloated child, his organs failing as tubes persisted in feeding him, cleansing him, driving his pink tender lungs to inhale, exhale. 'When it happened,' I said, 'all I could do was sit on his bedroom floor and wait.'

Teddy Lawson put his arm around me, resting the cigar on my shoulder so that the smoke circled my head.

'I'm drunk,' I said tiredly.

'Hey, we're all drunk.' He released me and made a grand, sweeping gesture with his arms. I couldn't think who he was including.

'So he was sweet on you,' Winnie joked on the way home. 'That explains it.'

From the back seat Jane said, 'I'm seeing double, goddamn it.'

'Listen, Jane,' I said. 'If you're going to go around at a third your recommended body weight, you might consider reducing your alcohol intake by at least as much.' Winnie and I exchanged a smiling look of camaraderie. I felt light-hearted and rolled down the window and sucked in the fragrance that arose from the bogs and thickets, from the tangled woods where lianas hung from the trees as though curtaining off secrets from the world of humans.

Yet, I thought, Teddy Lawson remembered sitting beside me at the cinema. How could he and I have burdened ourselves with such opposing memories of each other? Twenty years had altered him, and all my classmates, in much the way one January month had Rudy. The people we had become bore traces of the children we had been, but these traces were negligible – almost ornamental. Sometimes Rudy looked up at me from his chair and for a moment I caught just that: a curious, ghostly trace of the baby he had been.

In twenty years, who would Rudy be? In what manner would his memories intersect with mine?

The heavy foliage beside the road lurched gold and black in the headlights of Winnie's car. I was suddenly overwhelmed by too much life coming at me from the sticky black soil, the clicking insects and ferocious bird life. Behind the wall of trees along the roadside was a world that was no longer mine, and could not be had I wanted it.

I pictured Rudy in his bedroom, the air dry and overheated against the cold at the windows, and longed to be there now to kiss him as I did every night, believing that through this touch my memories could be erased.

'Life's a bitch,' Winnie suddenly offered.

Yes, I was about to say, it's one goddamn battle after another, but realized I no longer liked the dogged, angry bravery I had adopted as mine, or the woman it had made me. I closed my eyes tightly, as though the cigar smoke still stung them.

A VISIT
WITH OLD FRIENDS

I TELEPHONE MY MOTHER in the middle of the night and put it to her this way: 'What don't I know about Oliver Wyatt and you?'

Silence.

'When?'

'Yvonne …'

'When he was, like, seventeen? Eighteen?'

'Don't. Go overboard.'

'You know he's gay?'

'He was gay then,' she says. 'Don't you think?'

'You only had to kiss him.'

'Yes …'

'Go on.'

'Where are you?'

'Explain one thing to me, Mother.'

'No. A little voice is saying no. But don't forget, it was always you he liked.'

'Oh, please.' But what I'm thinking is what she wants me to think: it was supposed to have been me. He wanted me.

'You sound discouraged,' she says in a voice that makes me wonder how it is that *she* manages to sound so well. 'Why don't you and Rudy fly down? Spend the summer with me on the Vineyard?'

'He hates flying. He panics. Mother! Oliver Wyatt?'

'He was only three then.'

'I don't want to talk about Rudy.'

'He's a big boy now.'

'He won't swim. You know he's afraid of the water. I don't know what to say to you.'

'Yvonne,' she begins, then stops, perhaps considering what, exactly, she's willing to share with me. 'Let's face it, sweetie, those weren't easy times for any of us. I thought I was free as a bird and all that.'

I can hear the four of them still smoking and drinking it up in the other room: Jane and Oliver, a chuckle from Winnie. No sound from Tommy, but then he says little, anyway.

I hang up on my mother. I am not where she expects me to be, in the far north as Jane puts it, but next door. I have been next door all day, in fact, separated from my mother by only a small sweep of Nantucket Sound that floats before my mind's eye like a curtain.

That morning Winnie and Jane had been an hour and a half late, picking me up without apology at the Sweet Gale, a one-storey motel just outside Stokesley where I had spent a single night alone.

We were all tired. Jane was hung over. Winnie was driving, impatient with the traffic on Route 3, a spindly freeway appropriate to the population of decades past, now inadequately funnelling hordes southward to the beaches of Cape Cod. But the three of us were not interested in sand; we were visiting an old friend who had not appeared the previous evening at our twentieth high school reunion: Oliver Wyatt.

'I'm sure I'll be fine,' Jane told us, without prompting. She was in the front beside Winnie. Her perm, so beautifully defying gravity twelve hours earlier, sagged now at the base of her neck.

'Once you see Tommy,' I teased.

'Grow up,' she said so solemnly I was hurt. 'He's gay. People don't change.'

Winnie groaned and rolled down her window. She wanted to stop somewhere and light a joint. She had changed, I thought, without saying so. Shouldn't she be only a girl? Freckled, serious and bone-thin, weak from another water diet?

'Oh, Christ,' Jane whimpered, her head listing to the side.

'What?'

'Nothing. I'm hung over.'

I patted her shoulder.

'Although,' she admitted. 'You're right, he is something to look at.'

'I don't see it,' Winnie said. 'He's too quiet.'

'It's a matter of compatibility,' Jane whispered.

'Compatibility?' I said, finally irritated. 'He's compatible because he's gorgeous?'

Winnie hit the brakes as we approached the bottleneck before the bridge.

'It's always like this in the summer. Cape Cod is ruined,' Jane said in an elevated voice, turning her face to the side window to address me personally. 'You've been gone so long, Yvonne, you have no idea what's happened to our world.'

'Let's smoke up now.'

'No, Winnie,' Jane said. 'Not bumper to bumper like this.'

Winnie made a show of shifting her weight and directing towards me a severe raised-eyebrows look. I shrugged. I didn't care about getting high. It's never been a predictable business with me.

It took us fifty minutes to cross the Sagamore Bridge. The Cape Cod Canal lay strung out below us, as tepid and polluted as we felt. Winnie struggled with the other drivers while Jane sat suffering until at last she said to me, 'Got any antihistamines on you?'

'No. Why would I?'

'I thought you had allergies. Winnie?'

Winnie leaned over and fished around in her glove compartment.

'It'll knock you out,' I warned.

'Yeah, well, if I feel better.'

Ten minutes later she was unconscious.

'There's a joint in my change purse,' Winnie said to me.

'All right, but count me out.'

As soon as we pull into the driveway Oliver comes bounding out his front door and across the grass like an Irish setter. The house that rises behind him is a square, three-storey Georgian masterpiece with brick window-arches, Palladian windows and an elegant balustrade surrounding a nearly flat roof. He balances atop one of the white-painted rocks that separate his gravel drive from his level, close-cropped lawn, and tells us Tommy is just getting up and not decent. He fakes a look of astonishment, as though: how *unlike* him.

'Come on, let's switch cars,' he says, pulling us out and kissing us one by one. I'm so happy to be around him, I don't speak.

'What's the matter with ole Janie?'

'Well, she's hung over for one thing,' I explain.

'Those reunions,' he says. 'Killers.'

'How would you know?' I ask, to which he responds with a distinctive warbling giggle I discover I have missed.

'What Jane needs is a double hit of espresso,' Winnie says.

'No problemo. Get in my car. It's more roomy.'

I look at his car. 'A Mercedes?'

He's pleased. 'Get in the front, little miss.'

I smile and get in beside him, aware that I have dropped my guard as though it were a hot pan. Suddenly, I am the birthday girl, the only princess in town. Oliver always made us laugh. He intoxicated us with silliness, but also with the belief that all would turn out well. I might tell him anything.

'So? How was the reunion?' he asks once we're off.

Jane groans and Winnie says, 'You equipped?'

'I'm equipped,' he assures her.

'I don't want any local crap.'

Oliver smiles at her in the rear-view mirror. 'A girl after my own heart,' he says to me.

I giggle, like someone in love. But then I remember our single high school kiss as though it had happened last night: a taste-touch green with youth and doubt. And how quickly I had recoiled from it.

He has changed little. Put on some weight, that's all.

We stop at his beach house and drop off our stuff. It's small and likely cost a fortune. But beach house is a misnomer. Though it is surrounded by white sand, a small dune rises between the house and water, blocking out any view of the sea. Oliver leads us over it, through beach plum, purple vetch and shiny-leafed bearberry. We stretch out on the beach: rocky and brown and wet. Winnie and Oliver smoke up, but I wave it away and Jane dozes on her stomach, her face in the sand. The beach is deserted except for two teenage boys playing volleyball.

I watch the boys. Their faces are hard and expressionless as though only their deepest brain still ticks. As though they are so narrowed by concentration that there exists for them no greater design than exists for snowfall.

I think, how young they are. How much it matters to them that the ball go back and forth, aloft in the air over the net. On tiptoes and tight calves, they are unaware of the trio of herring gulls circling down, of Winnie and Oliver giggling, of the Atlantic Ocean moving up on the incoming tide with the momentum of bathtub water. Unaware that their futures are only minutes away.

'But what are they? Seventeen? Eighteen?' Oliver says when I try to express these thoughts aloud. He rolls over and digs his elbow into the sand and cups his head in his hand in order to study me, which pleases me. I remember – or rather, I feel – how each of us coveted Oliver's attention.

Jane is a school administrator, Winnie runs a community clinic, Oliver has his string of galleries. When he asks me what I do, I say, 'I'm a housewife.'

'Nothing wrong with that,' he tells me. 'I approve. It's old-fashioned.'

'You're a romantic, even still,' I say gently, not looking at him but watching that volleyball go back and forth, back and forth. But the words are not out of my mouth before I realize that I only want this to be true.

'She could have been lots of things,' Jane growls into the sand.

'Sit up, Jane,' Winnie tells her. 'You'll eat sand.'

'Leave her alone,' I say.

Oliver makes a noise like a cat and Winnie and I exchange a look of alarm, both of us seized by a sense of ourselves that we can't bear.

'Where are we going?' Jane mumbles.

'Where would you girls like to go?'

He takes us to an English tea house. Part gift shop and part patio restaurant under vast weeping willows and hanging pots of fuchsias. But once we are seated the proprietor and his wife won't leave Oliver alone. They hand him a photo album of their most recent trip home – an excursion down the English canals.

'Terribly slow, however. You'll understand, it was faster to hop off and stroll alongside. Wasn't it, Alexa?' He showers his wife with an admiring gaze.

Alexa puts a hand up. I take this to mean she did a lot of strolling. 'You know how these things are,' she murmurs.

Oliver flips through the photos, avoiding eye contact. Winnie clears her throat. Jane scowls openly at the pair. She's coming around, though still has that heavily medicated glaze. She is sitting slumped forward as though to shield sizeable breasts, which she does not in fact possess. Her eyes look dark and enlarged; the bags beneath them are somehow endearing. Her perm is smashed.

At last the proprietor and his wife tromp off and Oliver burrows his face in his palms.

'Regular pillar of the community,' Winnie says of Oliver, which we all, including Jane, find enormously funny.

A waitress arrives to take our orders and Oliver immediately snatches up our menus and says, 'You girls leave the ordering to me.'

'Tommy still working for you?' Jane asks, once the waitress has left.

'Yeah, Tommy's a permanent landmark.'

Which is what Jane really wants to know. Winnie and I exchange a smile.

Oliver begins moving things around the table with a distracted, fussy air. His face is ruddy, as though he gets regular exercise, but I think it's more from getting too much sleep.

'When the tea comes, Yvonne, I want you to pour.'

I nod, remembering the girl I was for him: emotionally uneven, but only enough to make me interesting, not risky or unsafe. But I wonder, now, if I had been correct in believing this; perhaps he would have taken the entire package that was me.

'Does Tommy smoke dope like you?' Jane asks.

Oliver looks up. 'Like what?'

'Like all the time?'

'Oh, Tommy's into whatever's on the go.' He glances around as though suddenly attacked by paranoia.

Then the cardamom buns, sweet tarts, scones and pots of jam and butter arrive. When I pour out the tea it drips onto the floral cloth and Oliver takes over, which is what he wanted all along. He wants to be me. But better. It's what he's always wanted. Not simply to possess me, but to be me. I feel a dull closing, understanding this. It seems that he has become, after all these years, more myself than I have.

'Is your mother still making those paper sculptures?' he asks.

'No,' I say, puzzled. 'That was years ago. She'd moved out by then. She was on Hickory Lane.'

'I know that. Listen, that paper she was into was pretty wild. Your mother, the hippie.'

'She wasn't a hippie.'

'One of the first hippies, yes. A flower child.'

'No.'

'Yvonne!' he scolds, surprised that I'm not amused. 'I used to get high with her.'

'No, you didn't. You got high with me.'

'You're impossible, Yvonne. I'm talking about later on. Is she still out on the Vineyard?'

'Yes. When did you get high with her?'

'Those paper things were works of art,' he tells Winnie and Jane. 'Because, Yvonne, I used to visit her on Hickory Lane.'

'Where was I?'

Oliver shrugs. 'College?' He has cleaned his own plate. He leans over and starts eating off mine.

'The far north?' Jane suggests.

I watch Oliver closely as he stabs my food. It occurs to me I might not tell him anything at all.

Hours later we're back at his beach house. We've had supper and picked up Tommy and are all high, even me. I spend a long time in the bathroom where I can't hear the rest of them, poking around in Oliver's stuff while keeping an eye on myself in the mirror.

I discover several brand-new toothbrushes in the medicine cabinet. I hold them in my hand, considering Oliver's instinct and common sense: toothbrushes for those weekend guests who have forgotten their own. Did he read about this in a magazine, or did he dream it up himself?

I picture my husband and son's toothbrushes in the bathroom in the country where I live, splayed by overuse, spotty with black scum. I am horrified with myself, with the poor comparison I make beside Oliver and his life, his toothbrushes and clean houses, his confidence and success. He has struggled; he is self-made; there are too many roles he has adopted and dropped, but at least he is here, rising three-dimensionally out of a one-dimensional past that once included me.

'We've been talking about you,' Oliver tells me when I reappear.

I concentrate on slipping back into the space on the sofa beside Winnie, across from Tommy. Oliver and Jane are perched side by side on kitchen stools as though leading a seminar. Jane has changed into a denim jumper and white knee socks.

'We think you're depressed,' Oliver continues.

'Give it a rest,' Tommy says.

It's the most uncomfortable sofa I've ever encountered. The cushion behind me is too fat, thrusting me into the room, but when I remove it I sink back too deeply. I tell myself it's just because I'm stoned that nothing is perfect. I return the cushion and look at Oliver. 'Why don't you talk about Jane? Jane loves to be discussed.'

'Janie can wait,' Oliver says. 'I'll get to her in a minute.'

Jane smiles, like someone with secrets she's happy to share.

'What does your husband do?' Oliver asks me.

I shake my head.

'How many kids do you have?'

I shake my head. 'I'm not talking to you.' I put up my hand. 'You got me too high.'

'What did she say? Two kids? Does she have two kids?' He looks at Jane.

'No, that's me.'

'And me,' Winnie reminds her emphatically, and at the end of a tunnel I wonder what it really is she means to emphasize.

Jane says, 'Yvonne has only the one boy. A peach.'

'A what?' Oliver asks, giggling.

'A sweetheart.'

'I'd like a couple of children,' Tommy says ardently. 'Four maybe. Two girls, two boys.'

'What's stopping you?' Winnie asks.

'Winnie!' Jane scolds.

'Boy, girl, boy, girl. In that order.'

'Oh, Tommy, you're so *symmetrical*,' Oliver says and we all laugh, except Tommy, who gives Oliver a look of sober disappointment, as though his lover has become both an imbecile and a stranger.

I take the cushion out again and sink back a few inches behind Winnie, whose body shields me from Oliver, and stare across at Tommy. He has wheat-coloured hair and a flawless tan; his bare legs are, without argument, extraordinary. He smiles at me, something I am not expecting, and suddenly I remember this: a spring afternoon in Stokesley twenty-some years ago, when the buds would have just been turning to leaf, the grass going green at its roots, when people would have been out circling their gardens, their tools cold and unfamiliar in their hands. Inside my house, Jane and I sat across from each other at the kitchen table. Winnie stood behind Jane, methodically applying ice to her earlobes. Oliver was somewhere behind me, until he was on all fours on the floor at my feet, too silly with hysterics to stand or speak.

'Oliver,' I said, peeved. 'You're too stoned.'

'It's … stuck,' he said.

'What?'

Jane and Winnie began laughing silently.

'The needle … I can't get it out.' He put a hand on the edge of the table and began hauling himself up. He looked so ridiculous I almost laughed too. I put my fingers to my earlobe. The needle was halfway through.

I had a fear in those days that people wanted to hurt me, one way or another, so I said, 'I'm going to kill you.' It was then I noticed my mother over at the sink washing her hands. She'd been out in the garden and there was mud on the linoleum. Her nails would have dirt under them for days.

'Oliver?' she asked, turning, in her voice that everyday annoyance. 'What are you *doing?*'

'So tell me something about yourself, Yvonne,' Oliver says.

I shake my head and put my hand up again. 'Never mind.'

'You don't work?'

'Was I shouting?' I ask.

'For Christ's sakes, she's totalled,' Winnie says to Oliver.

'Go to bed, Yvonne,' Jane says.

'There's an idea,' I say, not caring for Jane's dismissive tone.

'What?' Oliver asks.

I shake my head.

'Give it a rest, Oliver,' Tommy says.

I can see by Oliver's embarrassed, overworked face that he is running himself into the ground. That he is too old for this. Yet he presses on, saying, 'You're maddening, Yvonne. You know that? I'm *just* remembering that now.'

'She said, "There's an idea,"' Tommy explains to him in a calm throaty voice towards which Jane immediately pivots. 'Stop picking on her, why don't you?'

'I'm not picking on her. But she's just so prim. Prim as a primrose. Prim as a thistle!' he shouts, doubling over with laughter like a cartoon.

Jane's legs are going back and forth, her knees banging and parting, banging and parting. Her expression is one of exhilaration. 'That's right. Stop picking on her, Oliver.'

'Good ol' Janie. Always protecting Yvonne.' Oliver leans towards her, his lips puckered.

At this, Tommy moans, and throws himself into the back of his chair. In the silence that follows, I rise, suddenly forgotten and freed, though when I pass Oliver and he looks up at me and touches my arm, I see that Tommy has at last gotten through to him, has at last rescued him from the dizzying confusion of his high school antics, from a role that was the only one we ever knew.

Jane says to me, 'See you in the morning, hon.'

I wake hours later and realize they're still up in the next room. I can hear Jane, then Oliver, a chuckle from Winnie. I can't hear Tommy, but then he says little, anyway. My room is hot and suffocating, but outside a light shower begins and the fragrant air creeps in. Already, summer is here on the Cape.

I reach for the phone.

'Try to imagine, Yvonne,' my mother insists at last, blunt and tired. 'Finding yourself completely alone. Even if that was what you thought you'd wanted. I could never take the safe road. Not like … others.'

But this frank woman-to-woman stuff, it's nothing new.

In the morning I open the curtains onto Oliver's white sand yard and the hill of dune grass cresting under humps of clouds. Though I can't see the ocean I have a sixth sense that tells me it's there.

I'm reminded of the year my mother left Stokesley and Hickory Lane for good. Boxed up her home-made paper and equipment and took a house on Martha's Vineyard. I came home from college to help her move. She was lonely and I said I'd stay on a while with her there. We read mysteries, and in the afternoons biked down long straight roads bordered by a soft treeless landscape. We could sense the Atlantic Ocean near by, but were unable to see it. Then we got hot one day and abandoned our bikes and slid down the high dunes to a deserted beach. My mother kicked off her sandals and stripped naked and waded in, her shaggy hair light as grass on her shoulders and back. Eventually, I followed her.

My mother and I looked at each other over the crests of the waves and smiled. I imagined us transported by a strain of music only the two of us could hear. Later we sat naked on the sand and our bodies dried, leaving behind a crusty film of salt that suddenly, without warning or understanding, seemed utterly perverse. As though instead of being cleansed by the water, we had been made dirty.

THE BIGGEST MISTAKE

A SHAME Nicholas had that science camp, otherwise he could have joined them for the weekend. Bonnie said it was just as well, those Tercels are so cramped the kids would have been at each other before the overpass. But the moment he pulls up in front of Bonnie's house, Roy feels a jolt of homesickness for his son that startles him.

Inside, he finds they are far from ready. The lasagna Bonnie has made ahead of time so they don't have to eat out *every* night is still in the oven.

'Only twenty minutes,' Bonnie assures him, rubbing his arm as though she can sense his anxiety about moose in the road, about finding the key to the rental house under the flat rock at the entrance to the root cellar, about the rating this weekend will receive months from now, even years, when they all look back.

'I'm still in the process of encouraging Liza to pack, anyhow,' Bonnie says, then adds, her voice dropping to that tender notch, 'but Jacob is ready.'

Jacob is squashed into the very end of the chesterfield. There's nothing else on the chesterfield, but there he is shoved up into the end, hugging it as though the thing were crowded with people. His head is bent over his Gameboy, which Roy only now hears, a tinny sound difficult to call music. Although Nicholas owns a Gameboy, he is twice Jacob's age – Jacob is only five – and Sue severely limits his use of it.

Neither Roy nor Sue is a Newfoundlander. Over the years the tendency has developed between them to blame Nicholas's bad habits on this place. But Roy has been back home enough times, visiting nephews *and* nieces, to know that Gameboy addiction is not restricted to the island of Newfoundland.

Hooked through Jacob's arm as far as the crook of his elbow are two Sobeys bags stuffed with books, CDs, toys, some clothing. There's no point in talking to him with that thing going, and Roy doesn't want to interfere anyway, but he hopes Jacob has packed enough of the essentials: underwear and socks, bathing trunks, long pants in case it gets chilly, which it likely will.

He sits opposite Jacob to wait. He can hear the boy breathing irregularly, obviously influenced by his progress with the game. Even when Jacob moans and tosses his head back with disgust, he doesn't see Roy.

A door slams, then opens and Liza screams, 'I hate him! He ruined her hair. He ruins everything. I won't go. Not until he fixes her hair!' The door slams again.

For a moment Roy almost leaps up, thinking he must rush to defend himself. Although he recognizes Liza's deep suspicion of him, he has never heard her voice it so clearly. But it's Jacob. Jacob has done something to the hair on one of Liza's dolls – her wealth of them amuses Roy – and he relaxes, then notices that Jacob has not heard this uproar. Jacob's ignorance of his crime makes him seem so vulnerable, Roy whispers, 'Hey, Jacob?'

'Umm?'

Bonnie appears and says, 'Only five more minutes, honeybunch, and we'll be off. I just have to motivate Liza. Jacob, put that thing away immediately before I chuck it in the garbage and go help Roy pack our car.'

Jacob lifts his head and sees Roy.

* * *

Not long after the overpass, a car with a sticker of the Union Jack on its rear window overtakes them, and Jacob says, 'Look, Liza, the United Kingdom. That's where the Spice Girls live.'

Liza is still in a pissy mood. Jacob's mention of the Spice Girls is such a bad play, considering it was Scary Spice whose hair he cut, that Roy looks at Bonnie and they both smile.

Liza is brushing Barbie's hair. Roy notices how easily the stuff falls out. Her lap is covered with it. She says, 'You'd have to be living in the time of the dinosaurs not to know that, Jacob.'

'I'll tell you what people looked like in the time of dinosaurs,' Jacob offers, speaking in his robot voice: gravelly, flat and sluggish, 'They looked like monkeys.'

'Yes,' Liza says. Her voice is still clipped, but she's obviously beginning to forgive him. Roy glances at Bonnie and thinks he sees relief, which surprises him. 'And Jacob, billions of years from now, monkeys will look just like people.'

Roy nearly laughs out loud. He turns, ready to begin a discussion of evolution with Liza, whose intelligence stirs in him both respect and apprehension, when he catches the warning look on Bonnie's face. Roy looks back at Liza. She seems to be holding her breath.

'Is there anything that isn't difficult?' he asks, quietly, after a while.

'Come on now,' Bonnie says, touching him. 'There's plenty. Anyway, I thought you mainlanders never complained?'

'That's not what I mean,' Roy says, discouraged by the distinction she's made between them. He wishes she wouldn't do that.

They are passing through a long stretch of bogland that is green and yellow and shimmers with softness. Small groups of scrubby black spruce are scattered throughout and in the distance a range of low blurry blue hills seems to emphasize the flat, settled mood of this land-scape.

'Bogs, bogs, and more bogs,' he says, and Bonnie says, 'Those aren't bogs, honeybunch. Those are fens.'

'Let's play twenty questions,' he suggests.

'Fens, in case you're wondering,' she says, leaning towards him with that teasing smile, her fingertips drumming the steering wheel, 'are meant to have more grasses and stuff. See?'

'How do you know?'

'Someone told me.' But she glances in the rear-view mirror at her kids. Roy has met Bonnie's ex-husband: one of those guys who always has a field guide on hand.

'How do you play twenty questions?' Liza asks Roy.

He turns and starts explaining the rules: animal, vegetable or min-eral, yes or no questions, and only twenty noes allowed, though once they get started Roy drops the last rule. As he speaks Jacob and Liza stare out their windows, never looking at him, but he knows they're listening. So unlike Nicholas, who would be hanging off Roy's seat, too excited to follow and as a result, interrupting with questions.

Liza goes first. She starts with a mineral. Roy determines that it's located in the backseat and smaller than a breadbox, but then he runs into trouble. It's not seat belt or overhead light, not zipper or barrette or any piece of Barbie paraphernalia – not her diving gear or minute pots and pans. He shrugs and gives up.

'Give up?' Liza asks.

'No.' He turns and scans the backseat again. Nothing. He smiles at Liza with false embarrassment, as though inviting her to forgive him for his stupidity. Her expression is blank.

'Is it one of your fillings?' he asks.

'I don't have any fillings,' she tells him.

'Is it a rhinoceros?' Jacob asks.

'No, darling, it's smaller than a breadbox.'

'Okay, I give up,' Roy says. 'Give up, too?' he asks Bonnie.

'Oh, yes, I give up.'

Liza scoots forward and shoots her arm out between them in the front seat. She opens her fist to reveal a damp nickel.

'Very good!' Bonnie says. 'I would never have guessed that!'

'My turn,' Roy says, mentally switching from satellite dish to rear-view mirror, but not really minding because he can't help thinking how much better Nicholas is at this game. And Nicholas would never *hide* the item. 'It's a mineral,' he tells them.

'Is it bigger than a breadbox?' Liza asks.

'No.'

'Is it in Ontario?'

'No.'

'Is it a flying squirrel!' Jacob asks.

'No, darling, it's a mineral.'

'Is it in my house?' Liza asks.

Roy looks at her. 'No.'

She fails to narrow it down, and Roy doesn't help her. Bonnie has not been paying close attention, but when she suddenly asks, 'Is it in the car?' he lies and says no.

Liza bounces forward and says, 'That's twenty noes. You lose.'

Bonnie laughs. 'She was counting. You lose.'

Roy nods.

'We're almost there now. Only five more minutes.'

Dusk is coming on as they pull up to the house. Off to the side, across an open expanse that may be either fen or bog – Roy has no idea – lies the ocean. Bonnie turns off the engine and the first thing they hear is a whale breathing.

From the backseat, which seems suddenly remote and dark, comes Jacob's voice. 'Is it a bushbaby?'

'No, darling, the game is over.'

The house is set at the end of a lane, hidden below the main road. Roy feels a wonderful sense of isolation and a travelling backwards in time. It's a red saltbox with a front door that opens informally onto grass – not fieldstone or brick, wooden step or even gravel. In the back there is a shed that, although padlocked, is leaning at such an angle Roy feels he must warn the children to stay clear of it. The root cellar is easy to spot: a high mound of earth thickened with goldenrod, knapweed and nettles, and at its entrance a sinking, shrunken door. Directly in front of the door there is a flat rock, and here Roy stoops to uncover a single key. He feels like an archaeologist lucky on his first dig, although in his hand the key feels gritty, rusted, so that he doesn't want to think too much about getting into the house until he is certain that he can.

But the key works. The children run past him and Bonnie turns, saying she'll start bringing stuff in from the car now, and he realizes she too was waiting to see if the key worked.

Roy is first struck by the stale cool odour of mildew, then by the tasteless modernization the house has undergone. There are wall-to-wall carpets in every room, so old or cheap or both they have stretched and gathered into wrinkles in every corner. Jacob climbs into a stuffed chair covered with a yellow spread, and sinks.

Upstairs Roy finds the bathroom – more carpet – and three bedrooms. Although small, each bedroom has a double bed. He wanders from room to room, looking at things with curiosity and apprehension, as though he is still waiting to be welcomed in. The two rooms at the front of the house are larger and face the ocean.

He didn't realize how tense he was; suddenly alone he begins to shed the sense that everything is roaring and circling around him. There is such silence in the house; no cars, no TV, no refrigerator hum or disagreements. When he stops moving, nothing; he guesses they've gone outside again. He wants to stay upstairs as long as possible, where there is this dense funny atmosphere of privacy and voyeurism. He stoops before a window and looks for them, but they must have wandered around to the back. The distance to the ocean is more than he had thought, and there must be cliffs, for the strip of ocean – which has turned a dark grey – looks very narrow, even from here.

The next minute they're all coming up the stairs, Jacob and Liza lugging their Sobeys bags, Bonnie with a bashful, averted smile. When she whispers, 'How many bedrooms?' Roy realizes they have arrived at this place not fully prepared.

Jacob trundles past them and into one of the front rooms. He jumps onto the bed and says cheerfully, 'Okay, Mommy.' At the same moment Liza enters the opposite room and climbs into the centre of the bed where she stretches out.

Jacob begins jumping up and down on his bed, which makes a huge creaking sound, but when Roy says to Bonnie, 'Guess you and I will be taking this room,' pointing down the hall to the little room at the back, the singing stops and the creaking dies off like a ball bouncing down stairs. Using his robot voice, Jacob says, 'I want to sleep with you, Mommy.'

'That sounds pretty silly to me,' Roy says, and they all laugh.

But then Bonnie explains, 'Jacob sleeps with me, usually. If he doesn't start off with me, he comes in later.'

'You thought of this already,' Roy says to her.

'I'm not sure. Yeah, maybe I did.'

Liza is fast asleep hours later, surrounded in her bed by a dozen undressed Barbies and their wardrobes, when Roy says goodnight to Jacob and Bonnie and closes the door inside his little bedroom. The walls are pink and there is an orange bedspread; the single window lacks curtains, only a torn shade brittle as parchment paper. He hears the bed squeak in Bonnie's room, Jacob talking and Bonnie shushing. Then Roy becomes aware of Jacob standing on the other side of his door.

Jacob says, 'It's 11:08.'

'Thank you, Jacob.'

'Come back here, Jacob, and get into bed!'

But Jacob repeats this scrambling out of the creaking bed, presumably avoiding any lunge Bonnie makes for him, and scampering down the hall to stand on the other side of Roy's closed door to announce, 'It's 11:09.'

'It's 11:10.'

'It's 11:11.'

'It's 11:12.'

'Thank you, Jacob.'

'Jacob! Jesus Christ.' A larger creak and larger movements. Something is being taken away.

'Noooooo!' Tears.

And then Bonnie opens Roy's door and darts in. 'Sorry,' she whispers.

'No problem. Get in.'

But she stoops and says, 'Here. I'm hiding this under your bed.'

'What is it?'

'Shhhh! It's a clock. One of those old ones with the little flap, you know, that turns over with the new minute. *You know.* It makes a clicking sound each time. I think that's what he likes, the clicking sound.' She sighs and says fondly, 'What a torment, uh?'

'They all are.'

'Sorry, Roy. You miss Nicholas, don't you?'

'No, no. It's not that.'

'Look, tomorrow we'll go to the beach and the kids will leave us alone. You'll have a great time tomorrow, I guarantee it.'

* * *

What impresses Roy the most about the beach, and what will remain in his memory the longest – even longer than the image of that boy almost drowning – is the black sand. In truth, it is not black. If you take a handful and let it sift through your fingers, you see many colours: white, brown, beige, black, but mostly, many shades of grey. Still, Roy will like to say, *The sand on that beach in Newfoundland was black.*

They get there early and the place is almost deserted. Bonnie and the kids lead him down to one end where a small river is running into the ocean, cutting away straight banks of sand and creating safe shallow pools that Jacob and Liza play in for hours. Roy and Bonnie lie side by side, sharing a newspaper. After a while Roy turns over onto his stomach and dozes lightly, aware of Bonnie dribbling sand on his back. He feels a reconciliation with her, though there hadn't, really, been anything between them to reconcile, but knows that she feels it too. When he finally stirs and rolls over he is surprised by the weight on his back. A small mountain of sand slides off him. Bonnie laughs, seeing the look on his face, and playfully he grabs one of her ankles, then stops, 'Shit.

Where did all the people come from?'

'I know. Crowd's all here.'

By noon, people are packed within three to four feet of each other around the river and dogs are scampering about, yapping at strangers. Several jet skis are unloaded onto the beach and there is the odour of tanning lotion mingled with deep-fried food, which is coming from a take-out beside the parking lot.

'We're going to have to move,' Bonnie tells him.

Roy looks at her, surprised, and she says, 'One more Tilley hat and I don't know what I'll do.'

A number of Tilley-hat wearers are within earshot. 'They have got to be,' she begins, but he opens his eyes as wide as possible and she finishes in a loud whisper, 'the ugliest accessory on the go.'

'Where to?' he asks, a little ashamed of her.

She nods towards the other end of the beach. They haul the two kids out of the river and pack up and move. The peaceful, sheltered mood of the morning has disappeared. Both Jacob and Liza are hot, yet the ocean is too cold for swimming.

'No one's actually in the ocean,' Liza points out. 'They're all back in the river.'

'I want to go back to the river,' Jacob whines.

'Forget it. Too many people.' Bonnie stretches out on her blanket. 'Go on. Go play. Roy and I are having a conversation now.'

'I'm hungry,' Liza says. 'I haven't eaten anything since breakfast. That's three hours. What did you bring for me to eat, Mommy?'

Bonnie squints up at her daughter, who is standing close by with a wet, sandy Barbie dangling from each hand. 'We'll eat in half an hour,' she promises.

'I'm hungry, Mommy,' Jacob says, dropping onto his knees beside her. He takes the flesh on her upper arm between his thumb and forefinger and jiggles it.

Bonnie sighs and sits up. 'Hand me that bag,' she says to Roy.

Liza goes off, if not happily then politely, with a sandwich and juice box, but Jacob switches to his robot voice and says, 'I want something that begins with an "f".'

Bonnie reaches for the box of Froot Loops she has brought to the beach. Roy thinks of the outings Sue and Nicholas and he once took, and the small – but special – container of Cheerios Sue brought along. To Sue, food that children eat is either brain food or it is not. Froot Loops would not be brain food.

'No,' Jacob tells his mother. 'I want something else that begins with an "f".'

Bonnie looks around. 'Fig Newtons? I didn't bring any Fig Newtons, Jacob.'

Roy has witnessed this performance before. He finds it time-consuming and a little irritating.

'No!' Jacob cries, exasperated. 'This!'

'That's a peach, darling. It begins with a "p".'

'But it's a fruit. It begins with an "f".' Jacob is so disgusted he has abandoned his robot voice. He stomps off towards his sister.

Bonnie smiles, watching him go. When she turns to Roy he is looking at her, also smiling. He says, 'It's so obvious you love Jacob more than Liza.'

The change in Bonnie's expression to cold astonishment is so swift and absolute it unhinges him. He glances down the beach. More people are coming up this way now, and although no one is swimming, a few children are wading and one is going out in a rubber dinghy.

Bonnie reaches for her shirt and buttons it up over her bathing suit, then rises and walks to the water's edge. Roy lies down and closes his eyes. It's clouded over and the wind is up, but, as Roy is thinking, it was never a perfect day anyway. He rolls his head so he can see her, holding her arms around her waist with her shirt ballooning out at the back. He had noticed her on campus before he met her. One lunchtime when the two of them were heading the same direction and he was behind her. She was in a hurry, but she was pigeon-toed, and her quick wiggle was, although sexy, somehow absurd. She was wearing white sneakers and a dark dress – close-fitting and short. Her slightly bowed bare legs were sturdy and soft-looking, and her poise yet lack of self-consciousness bright and attractive. He would never have asked her out once they'd been introduced if he hadn't seen her that day, when he had believed he could know something about her from the way she walked.

She comes back now and stands a few feet away from him. He feels an insult coming, something he has never felt from her before. But she says, 'There's a boy gone out in a dinghy who can't get back in.'

Roy scrambles up and side by side, the two of them watch. Only now he notices the tight crowd of adults halfway down the beach, and the one woman who has waded out up to her knees, though she is wearing long pants, who must be the mother. Several hundred feet out on the water is a boy – ten or eleven years old – in a rubber dinghy paddling frantically in an attempt to get back in. But an offshore breeze is moving him steadily out to sea so that the paddling looks ridiculous from the beach.

'They better do something soon,' Bonnie warns.

The boy has stopped paddling and is flailing his arms. He is so far away now and the wind taking sounds out to sea, that his screaming is distant and fleeting, but it's not until Roy finally hears it that he realizes how out of his mind the boy is with panic. They watch as he jumps up and down hysterically in the little boat, his whole body punching it, and then as the paddle falls overboard and is quickly separated from the boat.

'That was a mistake,' Bonnie says. 'Now, just as long as he stays in that dinghy.'

Roy turns back to the beach. The knot of family and friends is still moving in and out of the water and Roy thinks if it were Nicholas he'd be swimming by now, despite the distance and water temperature and futility. Then he notices a man running towards the crowd at the river, where several jet skis are hauled out.

It seems to take so long for the man to get to the river, and when he does Roy almost loses sight of him among the people, and so long again to drag up someone who owns one of the jet skis. But not so long for that machine to cross the water in such a perfectly straight line it is a joy to see. As soon as the boy climbs out of the boat to sit behind the man the little boat lifts in the wind and flips end over end over end. The jet ski goes after it but Roy turns away. He doesn't want to know anything more about it. He wants to go home.

They shuffle back towards their blankets, kicking sand, dragging their feet. After a while Bonnie says to her kids, 'What was the biggest mistake that boy made?'

Roy feels depressed by this search for a lesson. So much like Sue.

'Letting the paddle get away,' Jacob says.

'That's right, darling.'

'The biggest mistake that boy made,' Liza says, 'was getting into that boat.'

Roy nods to Bonnie and without speaking the two of them begin to pack up. The truth about children, Roy realizes, is that no matter how you measure your love for them, you love your own best. The ease – the *grace* – with which this simple fact slides between himself and Bonnie makes Roy want to laugh out loud.

LANDSCAPE

I CAN HEAR MY SON Thomas crawling through the underbrush in search of hermit crabs. We've not had rain in the six months since we arrived and the woods are dry, carpeted with ochre-coloured leaves that rattle each time his knees push through them. A pair of quail doves whose world exists only between Billy's house and ours is scratching at the earth like chickens or small dogs. Lime dust rises around them. Above, leaves clatter from the trees like dinner plates as birds bombard the branches, seeking food.

But the hermit crabs are scarce. Staying put. And then there's the poison wood. I tried to warn Thomas.

The girls are at the beach, in bikinis, turning brown, though they are only eleven and twelve years old.

My husband's brother Billy is our only neighbour. He lives alone and drinks himself into his bed each night. People come down to these islands and disappear. It gets so hot my daughters sometimes long for the north, but after half a year the north is a place we have mostly forgotten. I have grown accustomed to the sandflies clustered on my pillow before bed, the nights my children and I meet in the kitchen to hold chilled cans of soda inside our opened shirts, rolling them down each other's backs. Rewarded when the breeze comes in off the sea, lifting the heat away.

* * *

We had been arguing since we left Ottawa.

When I told Jack I was tired, he said, 'We are *all* tired, Natasha. But only one of us is complaining.'

I wanted to lean across the aisle of that shuddering antique aircraft and punch him. Punch him and punch and go on punching until I felt better. But it would have taken too long and there were the other passengers.

And our three children. I can't remember where my daughters were seated, but Thomas was beside me. He was afraid of everything and held my hand. It steadied me, his small, limp hand in mine.

It had taken us three days to get that distance. The flight from Ottawa had been delayed, then forced to land in Miami where we got off and found a hotel. In Nassau we spent another night, Eloise throwing up, Thomas screaming at the sight of it, Jack fed up with us all and stalking out into the warm night. Though he came back with milk and sandwiches, I would not forgive him.

We came down hard in a field of grass. There was a whirl of noise and grey dust and I felt a stab of grief that Jack and I could not bear the sight of each other. For years we had threatened each other with promises of divorce. Instead, we were moving. And such an unexpected distance you might have thought something was chasing us.

I stood with my children and luggage outside the tiny airport while a grubby barefoot man eyed us with disapproval. The place emptied quickly, the few tourists getting into taxis and disappearing, the locals who had been hanging around as though this were the only happening place in town rising now and wandering off down the road. Thomas pushed against me.

'Where is he now?' I said. 'That idiot – that father of yours?'

Eloise and Sarah giggled with embarrassment. I knew they were anxious and scared but not so much that they couldn't hate me.

The barefoot man took a step towards us and said, 'He's making arrangements for a boat. Are you ready?'

He smelled of hard liquor. His yellow hair was shoulder-length and ratty, streaked with grey. He was unshaven and his feet were dirty, the nails brown and long. I took this all in quickly, the way you do if you're tired, over-watchful, but my eyes returned to his naked feet. There was litter, broken glass around, and the pavement would be hot. That's when I thought, those are not human feet; those are claws.

'Those yours?' He was pointing at our suitcases.

'Are you Billy?' I asked. When he didn't answer I picked up a suitcase and began to pass it to him but he hesitated, staring at my hand on the handle.

'Just set it down,' he told me, as though there could be nothing worse for him than accidentally brushing my hand. I put it down, and he hoisted it into the back of a white van.

In the taxi Jack turned to Billy, a brother he had not seen in nine years, and asked, 'Where did you sleep last night?'

'Don't know.'

Jack nodded. 'No surprises there.'

I was sitting behind Billy. His shirt was so worn a row of tiny holes was erupting along the seam at the neck. When I leaned towards him I was startled by his scent: metallic, but rooty, like something that lives underground. I saw that his hands were fists on his thighs and realized I would be afraid of every word that came out of his mouth.

Thomas began tugging at me and I sat back.

'Well now. What do you think of my brother?' Jack asked me later, after the long ride in a small boat across a turquoise sea never any deeper than twelve feet, its surface as sleek as a ballroom floor.

'A little stand-offish?'

Jack started laughing and had to sit down on the bed. Behind him were windows with neither screens nor glass. We were in our new home, one of two buildings set side by side where Jack and his brother Billy had spent their childhood.

'I'll have to tell him that one,' he said at last.

'Don't. I'd be embarrassed.'

'You? Embarrassed? Ice water runs in your veins, Natasha.'

'This house is a lot smaller than you described it, Jack.'

'It's exactly the way I described it.'

'Four bedrooms?'

'I never said four. I said two.'

'You're lying. You told me four bedrooms.'

He rose.

'Where are the screens for the windows?' I asked.

'Trust me, it's a lot cooler at night without screens. There aren't any, anyway.'

'I have to have screens.'

'Let me just tell you something, Natasha. When you shout, the whole island can hear you. Sound travels differently down here.'

* * *

I can see the top of Thomas's head as he comes up the path towards our house. His face is flushed. I meet him at the door and he stumbles in across the straw mats, tracking white sand.

'I thought I told you to stay in the shade,' I whisper.

'Miss Kitty says me and my sisters should be in school.'

'Where were you?'

'They have air conditioning in the school she says.'

'They do not. It's just a couple of goddamn fans.'

'Mommy,' he whines. He begins to tug at his clothes.

I pick him up so that he won't track sand through the house and carry him to my bed and lay a towel under his dusty feet to protect the bedspread and a wet washcloth over his forehead and eyes to settle him. I check for signs of poison wood and see that the rash will not be so bad this time. Then I kiss him up and down his hot neck until he pushes me away. We do this every day while Eloise and Sarah are off, shocking the island residents with their independence.

'When it rains,' Thomas says, 'I'll take a shower in it.'

'What a beautiful idea.'

There are wooden shutters for all the windows but it's too hot to close them. I said once how dark and stuffy it must be when it rains, blowing sideways, with the shutters down, and Billy said, Just you wait, you'll want to stay in bed all day it'll be so cold. He had almost smiled, saying that. I think now how dark it will be when the rain comes and the shutters are all shut.

* * *

After four months Jack left. I found Billy in the path that leads away from our two houses towards town. He was dipping his hand into a bucket of water and gently splashing the orchids seated high in the limbs of his trees. I watched as their aerial roots darkened and their spongy flowers nodded up and down, glistening.

'Jack's left,' I told him.

He continued at his work, the water running down his bare arm, and I could see that he already knew.

'There wasn't the work here he thought there'd be,' I said, moving closer to him, aware of his scent again, though understanding now that it came as much from him as from the woods around us.

'They see their own doctors here,' he said. The sunlight that reached his face was warm but the look he wore was wary and suspicious. I backed away, knowing that in some way I was offensive.

'But he grew up here. He belongs here.'

'No. He doesn't belong here.' He took up the bucket of water and began walking away.

'Well, the rest of us are going to stay,' I said, rooted to that spot in the path.

He stopped and came back towards me. We both found it difficult to keep our eyes on each other.

'I could rent that place if you left.'

'I have a right to stay.'

'Not if you divorce.'

'Who says we're divorcing.'

He made a loud, vulgar, disbelieving noise in his throat. It was my turn to walk away.

'But why? Why stay?' he called after me.

He was pleading with me to pack up and get out.

'I like it here,' I said stubbornly.

* * *

A grey-green bird flies into the house and perches on the bed near Thomas's feet. It's so small I could place it in my hand and close my fingers over it without causing harm.

'Black-faced grassquit,' Thomas informs me.

'I know,' I say.

'How?'

'You told me yesterday.'

'Eloise and Sarah aren't at the beach today. Did I tell you that?'

'Where are they?'

'They went with Miss Kitty to enrol.'

'School?'

'Do you mind?'

'What about you? Do you also have a secret plan to start school?'

'Is it really a waste of time?'

'It really is.'

We watch the grassquit fly down the hall to the kitchen.

'He likes our bananas,' Thomas says.

'And I like you.' I nuzzle into his hair. He smells of sand and dry heat, of burning wood and little boy. Then we rest, my cheek against his, staring at the wide palmetto frond that hangs just inside the room, lightly fanning the air. Vegetation presses up so closely the house could have grown here. I can barely circle the outside of it without being snagged by an orange vine or batted in the face by a small bird.

After a while we can smell the burning casuarina trees. A spicy smokiness. Billy has been burning his trees, trying to smoke us out, for weeks.

'Poor Billy,' Thomas says.

'He'll be sorry not to have a windbreak when it rains.'

'I might try school, Mommy.'

'I'll miss you,' I say, thinking that a person has to have someone to love.

* * *

We were here a month and I'd never been to Billy's place. It was less than fifty feet away, but not visible through the dense brush. Sometimes at the end of the day cooking smells came over to us. Grilled yellowtail or grouper, lemongrass, roasted peppers. He brewed his coffee in the evenings just as I was putting the children to bed. It had a tangy edge to it.

The children slept together in one room, Eloise and Sarah in the two small beds, Thomas on a mat on the floor between them.

One evening Thomas announced he could no longer sleep on the floor because of the scorpions.

'No scorpions this time of year, Thomas,' Jack said. 'Too dry.'

'There was one in Billy's garden this morning,' Thomas argued, reaching a hand down the back of his shirt and feeling around with it.

'You were at Billy's?' I said.

'They're rare, Thomas. And besides, they're not deadly. I've been stung. What do you think of that? Your own father's been stung.'

'They're deadly. Billy said.' Thomas pulled his hand out of the back of his shirt as though suddenly realizing where it was and turned towards me.

'Billy gets stung on average once a week,' Jack said. 'But only because he doesn't wear shoes. Deadly? He's teasing you.' Now Jack turned to me. 'This is just silly talk. Isn't it, Mommy?'

But I let Thomas sleep in our bed and when I returned to the kitchen, Jack was gone.

I fell asleep beside Thomas, listening to Jack and Billy's laughter carried patchily through the underbrush, imagining that I could hear the vines moving onto our house, criss-crossing the roof above me with a sound as distant as my own pulse underwater.

When I woke I could see the silhouette of Jack's body braced against the door frame and could hear his breathing and smell his breath. A night heron flew suddenly into the side of the house like a soaked towel thrown hard against a cement floor. It rose, screeching, towards the sea.

Jack took off his clothes and got in. He started to reach for me then felt Thomas between us. He rose and rested on an elbow. There was the sound of a boat zigzagging across the water away from the island.

I tried to stop thinking, to listen to nothing.

'You're awake, Natasha. I can see your eyes. Wide open.'

'No, they're closed.'

'Won't you even look at me?'

* * *

As I put Eloise and Sarah to bed they begin making demands. They have imposed a strict order to their room and I have been told not to touch anything, so I sit, admiring the treasures they have brought in from the beaches and woods and arranged on their bureau tops and window ledges.

'Rub my back, Mommy,' Sarah says. She is younger than Eloise and better remembers being my baby. But I am reluctant to touch her. She seems so grown-up lately. Inevitable changes have come to all of us here.

'Do the scratch thing,' she says. 'Rub and scratch, Mommy.'

'Only one minute left,' I say.

'That's not fair!'

'Oh! I almost forgot,' Eloise says, sitting straight up in bed. 'Miss Kitty says there's a ton of mail from Daddy waiting for you. The postmistress is going to send every last bit of it straight back to Canada if you don't pick it up tomorrow.'

'That's right,' Sarah mumbles into her sheets. 'Eloise is not lying to you.'

I'm less certain of the night than I am the day. The woods are never quiet and the sea pounds the limestone shore not far away. I can feel the vibrations as they travel through the hot earth to the floorboards beneath my feet.

So when I go out I don't go far, just for the night breeze. The branches of the bougainvillea brush against me like the paper arms of some friendly, other-worldly creature, all shadow and light, but I remember the colour of their flowers from the day: crimson with white centres.

Voices travel over from Billy's. Subdued, possessive. I think of Billy's toenails, so long they reach down and touch the dirt path as though seeking water.

The next day Thomas and I walk into town to get the mail. The post-mistress hands it to me without smiling.

Thomas asks that we stop in to see Miss Kitty, who sells baked goods from her back kitchen. When we get there a man is chatting with Billy in the doorway. When the man sees me the laughing drops from his face and his look is confused but hard. Billy walks away without a word.

Inside it is tiny and hot. Like a dollhouse cast into a fire. The small walls are blanketed with colour photographs of faraway places. Miss Kitty comes out of the kitchen and stands like a giant in her own home. I have heard she has grown children, yet she looks no more than eighteen in a green dress with Empire waist, short hem and puffed sleeves. Her blond hair is braided and lies coiled on top of her head. She stands on her massive bronzed legs and stares at me without expression.

'How much is the bread?' I ask.

'Two dollars, one loaf,' she says in a voice sing-song and elusive, so that the meaning comes to me like an echo.

I look beyond her into the kitchen. Blocking a doorway to the backyard is a card table piled with fudge, squares, pies, breads and rolls.

LANDSCAPE

'What about those?' I ask loudly, pointing at some tiny loaves, white with black specks. Thomas tugs at my hand.

'Coconut bread, just come out of the baker, three-fifty, two loaves.'

'I guess we'll have four then,' I say, looking at Thomas, whose eyes widen. 'And some fudge.'

When she hands them to me she smiles and pats my arm.

As we wander home I rifle through the mail. Jack has forwarded almost everything, as though he never looked to see what was there. The winter swim schedule, campaign pamphlets, coupons. A few letters from friends, notice of a high school reunion, the separation agreement.

'There's Billy up ahead,' Thomas says.

'Ignore him,' I say, then change my mind and move quickly to catch up with him.

'What the hell's your problem?' I demand.

'I've lived a long time without neighbours,' he says, walking faster. He's wearing jeans that drag around his bare heels in the dust.

'Get used to it.'

'I can't.' He stops in the road and looks at me. We've hardly seen each other since Jack left. The dust rises around us. 'Why aren't you tan like your children?'

'I stay in the shade.'

His eyes look bleary and hurting, but sober.

'It's hot,' I explain.

He throws the paper bag he's been carrying onto the dirt path. The loaf of bread slides out. 'Then why don't you leave?'

'I can't.'

* * *

One day before Jack left, I went across to the beach on the other side of the island with Eloise and Sarah and followed them into the sea. The saltwater was warm and clear as glass and suspended my body as gently as music. I imagined myself cast inside a glass marble, a swirling sea of blues and greens from which only my head emerged.

It was then I realized that I had been changed by this landscape. I thought, surely there is a landscape somewhere in the world for everyone. Landscape with the power to peel you away, strip of flesh by strip of flesh, until you understand nothing. Landscape like blind love.

* * *

Thomas comes down the path wearing yellow shorts with a blue seashell design I have never seen before and says, 'Billy, I think it's going to rain. Know why? I felt a raindrop.'

I look at Billy just as his hands drop to his sides. Wind moves through the undergrowth like an invisible hand.

The rain lashes, sideways. Inside the house, the shutters closed, I fold laundry in the kitchen in the half-light in air like a sauna, though I know that Eloise and Sarah will later refold theirs, rolling them into tight cylinders to keep out insects before packing them into their bureau drawers.

At nightfall Billy brings us candles. His feet are muddy with white sand. He puts the candles down then stands inspecting the room. My children are silent, watching him.

'I was renting this place for good money,' he says. 'Five hundred a week in the good months.'

'What do you need money for?' I ask. I watch his mouth, waiting for it to move again, to expose his white teeth. I picture him eating those foods I know only by smell, that I have never seen or tasted.

'By the way, I'm going back up north. To talk to Jack,' I say. 'Miss Kitty will stay with the children and get them across to school each morning. But don't worry, I'll be back.'

He sighs, as though this is the last straw, and looks past me to the outside, but the shutters are closed. I figure he doesn't want Miss Kitty around the place, hauling over her second-hand clothing and baked goods, then visiting him twice a day just to get a peek at his lifestyle.

There is a cold fog hanging over Ottawa. Jack is there with the car. He kisses me lightly, then suddenly holds me.

'We've had a miserable spring,' he says into my hair. 'How's it been down there?'

'Better than this.'

But once we're in the car Jack seems to recover and says, 'You can't stay there. It wasn't our matrimonial home and you've only been living there six months. Besides, Billy wants you out. I have to respect that. You don't have a leg to stand on, Natasha.'

After a while I realize the sky is white here, and Jack is crying. The heater in the car isn't on, but I don't ask why. I rub my hands together then shove them between my knees.

When I return a week later the orchids are in bloom: violet, tangerine, ashen-white flowers suspended high in the trees. The house is empty, and I hesitate, then make my way to Billy's. He's sitting in a beach chair among the stumps of his casuarinas facing the sea.

'There's no divorce,' I announce. Then I realize, of course, he already knows.

'Does this mean Jack will be around too?'

I am surprised by this, but he has not turned to look at me once and I wonder whether I have only imagined him speaking. On the flat stumps of the trees someone has placed a collection of rocks, feathers and shells. My children have been here. Suddenly I am sorry to have taken so much from him.

I turn, just as Miss Kitty emerges from the interior of Billy's house and stands there in his doorway in her green dress exposing her trunk-like legs, her eyes on mine. It's then I understand the folly of words here, and the order that reigns.

Billy shifts in his chair to face me. His collar is caught, turned under on one side of his neck: a second-hand orange shirt, new to him. Suddenly he laughs, a sound I have not heard before, with his mouth open. I see him lying over Miss Kitty, his ankles criss-crossing hers as though they have grown there.

That night I lift Thomas, despite his protests, out of my bed and lay him on the mat on the floor in his sisters' room. I have not seen my daughters all day, but I can hear them now, breathing in their sleep. I return to my bed and cover myself with a sheet.

Now that summer is here it is hotter than it ever was. Harmless grey spiders the size of a child's hand possess the top corners of all the rooms. Insects knock at the trees. Night herons thump the outside of houses up and down the island.

I hear him enter the house. He approaches without hesitating or asking, without lifting the sheet or undressing, and lies over me.

I shut my eyes, aware that the secret pleasure of this landscape is that it denies my mind access to both my past and future. But in the distance beyond my closed eyes I see myself and the immense place of craziness where I have crept, and know I am fortunate not to remember what it is I have lost.

A WALK IN PARADISE

MARY CATHERINE stands on the deck in pyjamas and sandals, listening to the fifteenth ring on the cordless. From within the barn emerge the sounds of radio and electric sander. These are the sounds that have awoken her. Not the gravelly hum of the fish plant generator across the harbour. Not her daughter Melody scraping a chair across the kitchen floor. Not – somewhere – a young gull screeching.

The bush peas in their boxes at her feet are collapsed with moisture and lie sprawled across the deck. Do they have some intention of travelling down the granite steps in search of a more sunshiny home? Over my dead body, Mary Catherine thinks. She's wondering if her father would like them staked, when he comes out of the barn.

'What's that bird making all the racket?' he asks her. 'Do you hear that, Mary Catherine? I don't know it.'

'A young gull,' she tells him, tossing the phone down at last. She walks to the end of the deck. The fog is so thick she could be underwater.

She sees what she has expected to see: on the roof of the house next door a young herring gull as soft and precocious as a kitten bobs ceaselessly and without grace. At the opposite end of the roof an adult gull is perched, ignoring the youngster.

The house is set as though in Mary Catherine's backyard, farther from the water but surrounded by more trees – red maples mostly – and is large for the island with three storeys, but even so, Mary Catherine is thinking, not quite large enough for the three women and six children who spend their summers there: Mary Catherine's two cousins, their mother – her Aunt Darby – and their children.

It takes her a few minutes to realize that her cousin Susan is outside, hanging wash in the fog. Mary Catherine marvels at her efficiency. At the hour she must have risen to have a wash ready for the line. An upstairs window is pushed open with squeaking complaint and Susan's sister, Georgiana, leans out in a green nightie, her yellow hair all over her face, and shouts across to Mary Catherine, 'Not foggy *again?*'

Mary Catherine smiles.

'Let's do *something* this afternoon. Even if it's just a walk to town. All right?'

Mary Catherine nods, then returns to her father, her sandals clapping loudly on the wooden deck.

'What did your brother have to say?' he asks her.

'No answer. Maybe he's not on the island.'

'What did Cindy say?'

'They're divorced now,' she says with exasperation, and certainly loud enough for him to hear.

'What?'

'I was right,' she says. 'About the gull.'

But her father has turned back to the barn. She hears the radio and buzz of the sander start up, while behind her in the house sounds indicate that Melody has dropped her cereal bowl on the kitchen floor.

She wonders where her goddamn brother has disappeared to. But she knows that the germ of her annoyance is not her brother, or Melody, or her father. Not yet, not really. She woke up annoyed. Found it waiting on her pillow.

At the end of every day, after her book has slipped from her bed, after she has watched through her bedroom window the fog lift for the night, Mary Catherine resolves to stop fighting with everyone. With her daughter, her father, her brother. Even her husband.

And every morning, like this one, irritation rises from its murky bottom and silently swamps her.

After lunch she stands with Susan and Aunt Darby at the bottom of the lane in the dirt space between her father's house and the barn, waiting for Georgiana who at the last minute rushed home to change her youngest one's diaper.

Mary Catherine looks around her, thinking they have been sentenced to a world whose permanent climate is fog. There is nothing that she can see except at close range, as she peers over children and nasturtiums alike in her struggle to identify them. And even then, everything is two-dimensional and dripping: dripping grass, dripping screen doors, dripping hair on the heads of children. The air is tangible and white. Panels of cloud stripped from another world and assembled around her.

At the top of the lane there is a cluster of children in helmets calling

impatiently. Mary Catherine recognizes Melody's voice, loudest among
them.

'CAN WE GO?'

'Just a moment, children,' Aunt Darby calls, so softly they hush.

Her father comes out of the barn. She realizes she has forgotten to
bring him lunch. His salt-and-pepper eyebrows droop with moisture
and he hasn't shaved in a week.

'Another busy afternoon for you women?' he asks sarcastically.

'We're walking to town, Uncle Bernard,' Susan explains. 'We're just
waiting for Georgiana.'

'I see. What do those kids up in the road want?'

Mary Catherine begins to draw her toes through the thin gravel,
making a rut in the direction of the barn. Her sneakers are soggy and
despite the moisture in the air, dust rises up and clings to them.

'They want to get out of here,' she says.

'So, Bernard. What are you working away on there in the barn?' Aunt
Darby asks her brother.

'Sanding.'

'Sanding what?'

'Boards.'

'Boards for what?'

He exhales as though he wishes his breath could send them all away.
'Mary Catherine?' he says, but when he lifts his head he cannot find her
in the fog.

'Behind you,' Susan says.

Mary Catherine has drawn her rut all the way back to the entrance to
the barn. 'What are you doing?' her father exclaims. 'Now someone's got
to come rake over that. I just had new gravel brought in.'

'You're losing your marbles, Bernard,' Aunt Darby says, and Mary
Catherine freezes. 'There's not enough gravel here to fill a sandbox.'

'Another busy afternoon for you women?'

'CAN WE GO!' Melody screeches from the top of the lane.

Georgiana comes barrelling across the lawn, moving quickly on her
strong legs, her daughter Lily bouncing on her hip like a bag of
groceries.

Georgiana and Susan are athletic-limbed and golden. Mary Catherine looks nothing like them but has spent good portions of her life

wishing she did. She wonders if they realize how they glow in this fog, how they are easier to see than other people. She imagines herself, with black hair like her father and daughter, emerging from the fog no more spectacularly than a wet tree trunk.

Georgiana whips Lily off her hip and struggles to deposit her in the stroller. 'Just an hour of sun,' she says. 'That's all I ask for. One hour.'

They start up the lane, Georgiana and Susan both pushing strollers, Mary Catherine's free arms hanging stiffly.

Lily squeaks, 'Down, down,' and begins backing out of the moving stroller. The children waiting at the top of the lane mount their bikes.

'CAN WE GO!'

'Yes, yes,' Aunt Darby says, waving them away.

'Lily, get down! She's not eating any more of those apples, Mother. I'm spending a fortune on diapers.'

Susan rolls her eyes and says, 'It's just a diaper, Georgiana. What's your problem all the time?' She looks to Mary Catherine for confirmation, and Mary Catherine forces a smile.

Aunt Darby touches her and says gently, 'He's not himself today. Are you all right?'

'He's fine. He's cranky.'

'At least he's put on a shirt.'

'If you can't cope with four children,' Susan calls after her sister, 'you should never have brought them into this world!' But Georgiana has raced her stroller up the lane to the road. 'She should have stopped at two. Like me. What's she trying to prove?'

'Mother!'

'What is it now, Georgiana?'

'I hate them on those bikes,' Georgiana says when they catch up with her.

'Why?' Aunt Darby asks in that astonished, precise voice of hers that Mary Catherine loves. 'Why, for heaven's sake, Georgiana?'

'I just do, Mother.'

Day after day, Mary Catherine thinks, fog and drizzle. Rain and cold. Long pants, soaked sneakers. Everything damp. Inside the white clapboard house she shares with her father and daughter, and with her husband on weekends, there are odours that best belong in cellars or suffocating beneath banks of seaweed.

'I'm not worried about the bikes,' Susan says to Mary Catherine. 'Are you?'

Mary Catherine steals a look at Georgiana. 'No,' she says to Susan. 'Of course not.'

The centre of town is a three-minute walk away. The children are biking towards it, all over the road.

'Everyone! On the right-hand side of the road!' Georgiana shouts.

'The sidewalk is safer,' Aunt Darby points out, though the sidewalk is on the left-hand side.

Mary Catherine hears voices behind her and turns. Three boaters dressed head to foot in yellow foul-weather gear are strolling up, gaining on them. One of them says, 'You have a beautiful island.'

'The right, Mother! They should always bike on the right. They have to learn –'

'Georgiana!'

'Mother!' She stops, and Lily immediately scrambles out of her stroller and sets off marching down the road, her left arm swinging wildly out of sync with her right, her diaper drooping off-centre. Only Mary Catherine seems to see this. She is touched by the child's yearning to be one of the big kids.

The boaters begin a wide detour around them.

'Must you always contradict everything I tell them?' Georgiana screams at her mother. 'I tell them one thing, you tell them the other.'

One of the boaters glances over her shoulder; all three quicken their pace. But Georgiana, Aunt Darby, Mary Catherine – even Susan – are suddenly grinning. There is a certain pleasure, Mary Catherine thinks as they walk on, in making a scene. Yes, here is a pleasure to wake up to.

'Has he called?' Susan asks Mary Catherine.

'No.'

'So you don't know if he's coming this weekend?'

'No.'

'I'm sure he'll call. Right? Eventually.'

'What is it with you girls?' Aunt Darby exclaims. 'Why is it so impossible for you to get along with your husbands?'

The children have reached Main Street and are waiting at the stop sign, all shouting at once for the go-ahead to cross over.

'I hope no one's trying to take a nap,' Mary Catherine says.

'A nap? Who takes naps?' Aunt Darby says musically. 'On a beautiful day like today?'

'CAN WE GO? CAN WE GO?'

'Yes, yes.'

'Walk your bikes on Main Street. It's the law.'

They cross over in a tight cluster and coast up onto the sidewalk. Georgiana's son Peter crashes into the outside of the electric company office.

'Oh. My. God,' Georgiana says and Mary Catherine recognizes in her cousin's voice that whine of exasperation that only a mother can produce: that certainty that she will not survive one more fall-down, bloody knee, stubbed toe, broken bone or set of stitches.

Peter rises wailing from beneath his turquoise bike and into his mother's arms. Georgiana turns and looks steadily at her mother for several seconds.

'Oh, what's her problem!' Susan cries.

'It's his bike,' Georgiana says. 'I hate his bike. He can't ride it.'

'It's brand new!' Susan tells her mother.

Lily has marched ahead. Mary Catherine takes charge of her stroller. 'Move,' she tells the children. 'People can't get by. Move. Walk your bikes.'

'I want to ride it,' Melody insists. She's straddling her bike, one foot ready on the pedal, giving her mother a look there's no getting around.

But Mary Catherine says, 'Not on the sidewalk, honey.'

'Yes. I want to. I will.'

Susan is behind Mary Catherine with her stroller and in it, her three-year-old daughter. Up ahead Susan's five-year-old daughter is walking her bike. Sometimes Mary Catherine and Georgiana joke that Susan drugs her children.

'Why is everything World War Three with her?' Susan says.

Mary Catherine knows the competition between Susan and Georgiana will never end. There is no solution, no peace plan. But she says, 'Susan, your children are angels.'

'I'm sick of hearing that.'

Up ahead Aunt Darby snatches Lily just as she heads out into the street. Lily squirms viciously in her grandmother's arms. 'Down, down. Me down, Mommy.'

'Oh, this child,' Aunt Darby says.

'Down, Mommy,' she squeaks again, looking now at Mary Catherine, who smiles, and Lily gives a gummy grin in return.

In front of the post office Mary Catherine runs into her brother.

'I've been calling you and calling you,' she says. 'We have to talk. Where have you been?'

'Yup, yup,' he says, backing off. He's handsome but pale, his face long and unpredictable this summer. It worries and frustrates her to see him.

'He can't stay another winter here alone,' she says. 'You and I need to talk. We need a plan.'

Brakes screech behind her and Mary Catherine spins around, but it's just some woman crossing Main Street without, apparently, looking first. When she turns back to her brother, he's gone.

All the bikes have been propped against the outside of the grocery except for Melody's.

'I want to ride it,' Melody says when she sees her mother.

Aunt Darby is inside the hardware store ordering Peter a new bike. 'I hate his bike,' Georgiana explains to Mary Catherine. 'He doesn't know how to ride it.'

Susan rolls her eyes.

'Why can't I ride my bike?' Melody shrieks.

'Listen, will you just. Be quiet.'

'You were going to say shut up, Mommy. You almost said it. I'm telling Daddy.'

'She was up too late last night,' Mary Catherine says to Georgiana, because she knows she will understand and because if she doesn't say something she's going to grab Melody and shake her. 'That stupid movie the baby-sitter let her watch. She's exhausted. Look at her.'

Melody is glaring at her mother. Suddenly she stamps her foot and throws her bike down.

'Oh my,' Susan says, looking away.

Aunt Darby comes out of the hardware store and freezes.

'Is there anything anybody actually wanted downtown?' Mary Catherine asks. 'Is there a reason we're here?' She turns to Susan but

Susan stares at her without speaking. And Aunt Darby and Georgiana are giving her funny looks. No one is moving.

'Would your girls eat spaghetti if I made it? Susan?' Mary Catherine asks. 'What *is* it?'

Susan looks past her and says, 'Hello, Cindy.'

Mary Catherine turns. The woman nearly hit by a car is coming up the sidewalk. 'Oh, Cindy, hi,' she says, understanding now her brother's hurry to get away.

'Hi, Mary Kay.' She sounds friendly, but her pace doesn't slacken.

'How's everything?' Mary Catherine is smiling so hard her cheeks feel sliced.

'Okay.'

'That's great.'

Not until she has passed and gone on does Mary Catherine register the change in her sister-in-law: evasive, haggard, a little unwashed.

Mary Catherine stares at the sidewalk as her aunt and cousins circle in. She wonders how it happened. Was it something specific? Some difference that arose between the two with the drama of an unforgivable crime? Or was it more sweeping? A widespread shutting down of all their tender feelings? Mary Catherine would like to know. She would like to know at what moment her brother and his wife said to each other: go away from me now, enough is enough. She realizes they frighten her.

'I'm glad you spoke to her,' Aunt Darby says.

'I didn't even see her, you know. I bet she thinks I was avoiding her.'

Aunt Darby nods, a little amused. 'Yes, well, it's all you can do. You girls think you can change the world.'

'The three of you saw her'

'Divorce is hard on the whole family. Especially on children.'

'They didn't have children.'

'I'm speaking in general terms.'

'Yes, we'll come for supper, if you were inviting us,' Susan offers, and Mary Catherine smiles at her gratefully and says, 'Okay, just let me pick up another box of spaghetti.'

But when she takes the box off the shelf the end opens and the contents empty onto the floor. A couple of salesgirls appear and begin picking the noodles up one by one, cracking jokes. Mary Catherine stoops to help them.

Two women wander down the aisle and wait, though it would be faster, Mary Catherine wants to point out, if they turned and went down another aisle. She glances up at them. One she recognizes. She's been introduced to her half a dozen times over the years, but acquaintances like that slip away so easily on this island. No one really wants to keep them, summer to summer. The other is a visitor. She's wearing stone-washed jeans that are crisp and dry, sandals that are not soaked through, the leather not yet ruined.

'I'm sorry the weather isn't better,' says the woman Mary Catherine recognizes.

'The weather? Take a look around you, Maggie. Look at the quaint little houses. The glorious salt air. You cannot, and I do not lie, f–ing breathe in the city this summer.'

'I guess it's the heat on the mainland giving us all the fog,' her hostess says weakly.

'This is paradise, Maggie. Why didn't you tell me?'

Mary Catherine stands and pulls another box of noodles off the shelf.

There's a long line at the checkout. Melody appears. 'Can I get something? *Please?*'

Mary Catherine picks out a pack of cherry gum. She wants to get rid of Melody before some difficulty arises between them.

'There are only six pieces in this, Mommy.'

'There's six of you.'

'What about Lily? What about Lily? What about Lily?'

'Melody!'

'What about Lily!'

'Oh, right, Lily. Now listen, just don't let her see it. Do you understand?'

'Yes, yes, yes.'

'Don't let her see it, Melody.'

They wait in line. Melody puts the gum on the counter but the cashier is in conversation with the cashier behind her. 'That was not my idea. I told them before –'

Mary Catherine picks up the gum and says loudly, 'Could you ring this in now?' The cashier looks at her, startled only for a moment. She rings in the gum and Melody runs outside with it.

Mary Catherine inches the noodles along, but the cashier has turned again. 'I told them. Tonight, I ain't available.'

Mary Catherine examines the girl's sprayed hair pulled every which way over her head and fastened with too many ribbons and clips to count. She looks ridiculous, like a pony for a show, and those contraptions in her hair, they look like small pitchforks or some other antiquated barnyard tool. Mary Catherine is dying to tell her this.

Outside everyone is chewing gum except for Lily, who is going up to the children one by one and pleading, 'Me gum. Mommy, gum?' She's wearing Peter's helmet, which is too big and covers her forehead and one eye.

'She's too young for gum,' Susan says. 'You'd have to be insane to give a child that age gum.'

'Will one of you please give her a piece of your gum?' Georgiana begs.

'I'm sorry, Georgiana,' Mary Catherine says. She stares at the chewing mouths, suddenly suspecting that if the fog were to vanish in the next minute, and the sun come streaming down, it would make little difference. That it would take more than that.

'Please,' she says to the children. 'That line in there is from here to tomorrow.'

Susan's five-year-old daughter comes forward. 'I'll give you some gum, Lily,' she says, but Lily turns and scurries into the grocery.

Mary Catherine goes after Lily, moved by the sight of that bagging diaper and engulfing helmet, and sweeps her up just as she begins rummaging through the racks of candy bars and gum.

'Me gum, Mommy, me gum?' she squeaks and Mary Catherine hugs her. She weighs so little and Mary Catherine remembers the precise loveliness of this size child.

Outside, Susan's daughter removes her gum from her mouth, tears off a piece and hands it to Lily, who pops it in her mouth. Susan makes a face but says nothing.

Lily is making straight for the street. Georgiana grabs her and tries to stuff her legs into the stroller. 'The policeman is going to be upset if you run all over Main Street, Lily. Stay!'

'The policeman is drunk,' Melody says. 'Daddy said.'

'Down, down. Me down, Mommy.'

'Don't ride your bikes on the sidewalk!' Georgiana shouts.

'What happened to your mother?' Mary Catherine asks.

'She took off.'

'Can you blame her?' Susan says, her buttery face deformed by anger. Even her golden hair seems suddenly snarled and unkempt, as though it too takes a beating from this rivalry.

Once off Main Street they leave the crowd behind. Side by side, Mary Catherine and Georgiana walk between clapboard houses and trim, boggy lawns. Purple loosestrife growing in the ditches alongside sags with black moisture. Mary Catherine imagines the children racing down the lane and pulling up beside the barn, her father appearing just as the bikes are thrown onto the sparse gravel inches from his dahlias.

Susan is several yards ahead.

'Why is she so jealous of me?' Georgiana asks. 'Me?'

Mary Catherine wants to say, it's just something that is. Like panels of white fog. Like her father forgetting each of his mornings at the end of each of his days. Like divorce. But everyone, even Georgiana, wants more. So she says, 'Her children are angels.'

'That doesn't make any sense.'

But it does. Mary Catherine knows that, somehow, it does.

She stands at the barn entrance until her father turns off the electric sander and raises his wobbling head.

'Your husband's been calling for you all day. I said I didn't know where you were.'

'We walked to town.'

'Well, I didn't know. You could have gone over to Blue Pond Island for all I knew.'

She's wondering how she's going to get those trousers off him tonight and into the wash, when suddenly he takes a step back, deeper into the barn. 'Have you seen your brother today? If there's a problem, he should come to me.'

'How's it coming?' she asks, gesturing vaguely.

'What's for supper?'

'Spaghetti. I invited Susan and her girls. I have to, Dad, every once in a while,' she says, seeing his look. 'Anyway, they're angels.' But he doesn't understand this remark, how funny it's becoming. He's giving her such a savage look she realizes he could be thinking anything. She could be anyone.

But then he makes his way slowly around the smooth planks and puts a hand to her cheek. She feels the sawdust rubbing off onto her face. 'You were the only angel I ever knew of,' he says.

'Daddy,' she says.

'He's been calling all day.'

Upstairs she scouts for Melody but, unable to find her, sits before an open window where the mildew smell of the house is weakest, and picks up the phone.

'How's paradise?' he asks.

'You've been calling all day?'

'Is that what Bernard said? I called once.'

'So?' she says, a little rudely, then looks out on the cool summer day and for a moment forgets everything. Beyond grass that is such a vibrant, luscious green it could be velvet there is the strip of yard running wild with blackberries and goldenrod, and beyond that, the flat harbour: a plate of lobster boats all pointing one direction.

'So? Mary Kay?' He lowers his voice as though he's surrounded by colleagues and cupping the phone tightly to his mouth, but she knows this is not true: his office door is closed; he's alone. He simply wants her to feel his effort, that she is worth his special care. He says, 'Let's not fight.'

She nods, agreeing, but then doesn't hear another word he says. Paradise, she is wondering, would paradise really be a place any of them would want to live, even if they could?

Some of the stories in this work originally appeared in the following publications: 'Reunion' and 'Boat Ride' in *The Fiddlehead*, 'Sunken Island' in *Pottersfield Portfolio* and *Journey Prize Anthology 11*, 'Movie Children' and 'The Biggest Mistake' in *TickleAce*, 'Cruelty' in *TickleAce* and *Journey Prize Anthology 10*, 'Winston' in *Grain*, 'A Walk in Paradise' in *The Malahat Review*, and 'Three Weeks' in *The New Quarterly* and *99: Best Canadian Stories*.

Originally from Massachusetts, Libby Creelman now lives in St. John's, Newfoundland. Her short stories have been published in literary magazines across the country and have been selected for *99: Best Canadian Stories* and *The Journey Prize Anthology*, numbers 10 and 11. She is a six-time winner in the Fictional Prose category of the Newfoundland and Labrador Arts & Letters Competition.